The Worlds Of Evad™

Throughout The Vastness Of Space

Volume 1
The Alpha Missions

<u>Concept and Story by:</u>

David Richmond

<u>Author's Notes:</u>

The Worlds Of Evad™ is dedicated to:
Stanley, Jean, Paul and Roxane Richmond
for their love, support and encouragement
towards my explorations of my visions.

Special Thanks to: J. Daniel Roland – Roland Music USA
for without whom the *complete* scope of this series
would not have been possible.

Published by: Evadware Productions, Ltd.
P.O. Box 374
West Seneca, NY 14224

ISBN: 978-0-578-04875-8

Printed in the United States of America

.00
Mission Briefing

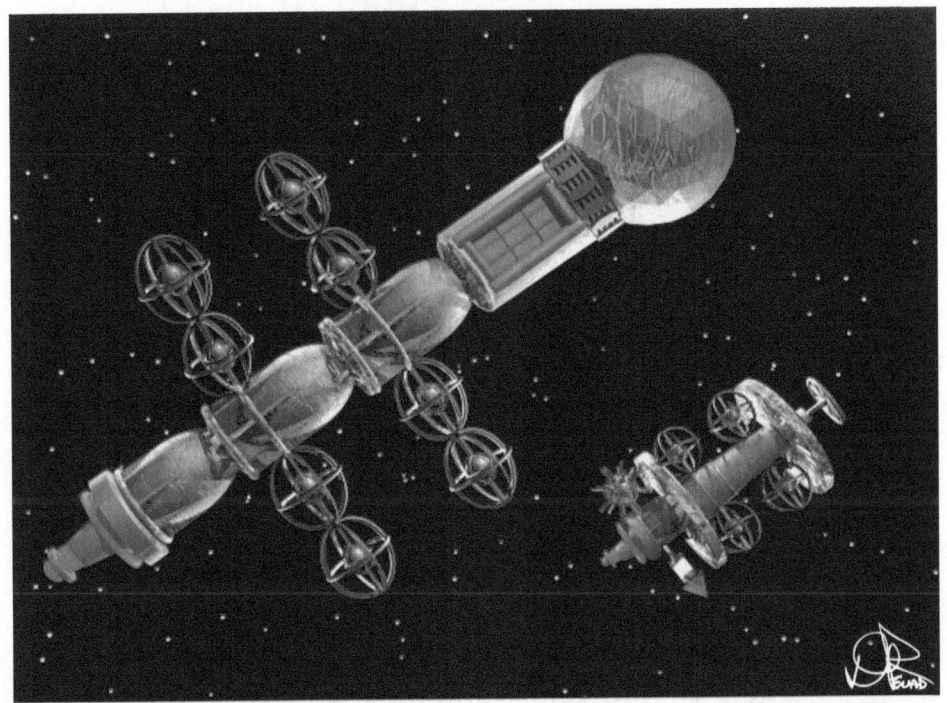

It is the future...

Shortly after the last military aggressions between three of the world's super powers, a conflict that redefined the traditional definition of war, as it lasted but a day and consisted of a single strike and counter-strike, leaving the three nations involved, virtually erased from existence, the scientists of the world gathered and unanimously agreed that an aggressive plan was needed to explore the vastness of space for additional inhabitable worlds, that humankind could colonize in order to help ensure the continued existence of our species, should the remaining governments of the world fail to learn from the mistakes made that fateful day in humankind's history.

It is the 43rd anniversary of the formation of the Deep Space Exploratory Consortium (DSEC). The DSEC was formed when scientists of all disciplines from around the world met with the leaders of the remaining world governments to propose the consolidation of financial resources and technology towards a unified exploration of space for the benefit of all humankind.

Forty-three years ago on this very day, after nearly a year of scientific presentations and intense governmental deliberations, due to the enormous resource requirements associated with the exploration of the vastness of space, it was agreed that a unified effort was the most logical approach, towards undertaking this daunting quest, as well as, bringing the remaining governments together towards unifying humanity as a species.

As the vastness of space made designing a mission to "see it all" impossible, the DSEC developed a plan that was agreed to by the majority of its members and hence, the development of the intergalactic exploratory probe Evad began. The design and implementation of probe Evad's construction took just over 18 years.

The intergalactic exploratory probe Evad was the first totally autonomous, most sophisticated and largest spacecraft ever constructed by humankind. As its enormous size made launching it from the surface of the Earth virtually impossible, the members of the DSEC unanimously agreed to update and expand the currently orbiting International Science Space Station and assemble probe Evad in low Earth orbit. The update to the Science Station included the eventual addition of the Uplink Transponder Dish (UTD) for communicating with the Transponder Array Complex (TAC) that the DSEC would come to agree should be constructed on the surface of the Moon. The UTD would become not only the largest Transponder Dish ever put into orbit, but, would also become the largest single 'non-Array' Transponder Dish ever constructed. At the opening ceremonies to begin the Science Station renovations, the Science Station was officially renamed "The DSEC Spaceport".

Due to probe Evad's enormous size and unprecedented number of component parts, as well as the materials that were needed for the renovations to the Space Station, each participating government averaged six supply mission launches per year, which resulted in a staggering 2,052 total launches in order to put into orbit all of the necessary materials and supplies required for the construction of probe Evad and the conversion of the Science Station into The DSEC Spaceport.

Probe Evad consists of three main modules; at the front of the craft is the scanner array, which contains a spherical array of both short range, as well as long range scanners, that allows probe Evad to scan the Universe in nearly 360°. The scanner array consists of over one thousand uniquely specialized scanners, giving probe Evad the capability of scanning for every type of elemental compound known to humankind at the time of its launch. The spherical array is protected from anticipated spatial debris impacts, as well as from attacks by unknown potentially hostile alien life forms, by the combination of the multifaceted, spherical, titanium and carbon-composite-fiber reinforced shell that encompasses the array and the electrostatic force field generated by probe Evad's power module that protects probe Evad in its entirety, which is capable of withstanding a single impact equivalent to that of a one megaton blast.

Directly behind the scanner array is the fabrication module. Due to the extreme velocity and linear trajectory that was preset when the intergalactic exploratory probe Evad was launched, the fabrication module of probe Evad will assemble and release sub-probes to investigate points of interest along its preprogrammed path throughout the Universe.

The fabrication module is truly one of the most remarkable technological accomplishments by the DSEC, literally a concept born from Science Fiction. Utilizing sophisticated holographic lasers and incredibly advanced 3-D modeling computer systems, the fabrication module can convert the energy probe Evad's power module generates, into physical matter based on the constructional models stored in probe Evad's enormous onboard database.

Unlike probe Evad, which has on-board power recharging technologies, the sub-probes are only equipped with short-term power modules, limiting their exploratory capabilities. The sub-probes are also deployed with minimal defensive capabilities. Probe Evad can, however, alter the size and mission capabilities of each sub-probe based on independent needs analysis of points of interest as they arise. While countless configuration variations are possible, there are three main capability levels of sub-probes.

A Level 1 sub-probe, the smallest and least sophisticated of the three classes of sub-probes, is only equipped with minimal engines, generally intended to establish a gravity assisted orbit around the world it's sent to investigate. As Level 1 sub-probes will typically be deployed to investigate worlds where probe Evad's long range scanners indicate minimal chances of there being intelligent life forms, they are also therefore only equipped with basic bio-life scanners and minimal language interpreters, compilers and communication systems. They are however equipped with full-range topographical scanners and sophisticated atmospheric, chemical and molecular analytical systems.

Level 2 sub-probes are equipped with twice the matter collectors for power generation than that of a Level 1 sub-probe. Level 2 sub-probes are also equipped with full-range bio-life and topographical scanners, language interpreters, compilers and communication systems, as well as, the full compliment of atmospheric, chemical and molecular analytical systems. Level 2 sub-probes will be deployed to investigate worlds probe Evad's scanners determine to have a likelihood of intelligent life forms and their more powerful power systems give them a longer life-span, as well as, greater maneuverability, allowing them to alter their orbital positions, as well as, to freely explore the planetary systems to which they are deployed.

Level 3 sub-probes, the largest and most sophisticated of the three classes of sub-probes, are deployed to planetary systems that probe Evad's bio-life scanners indicate high levels of bio-activity and therefore the greatest likelihood of intelligent life. They are equipped with extremely powerful language interpreters, compilers and communication systems and their standard four matter collectors are supplemented by small fusion reactors providing extended power generation capabilities, giving the Level 3 sub-probes extremely long life-spans. Level 3 sub-probes are also equipped with deployable mini-probes capable of landing on the surface of worlds greatly enhancing the Level 3 sub-probes various analytical scanners. Of the three levels of sub-probes, the Level 3 sub-probes are the most maneuverable and have extremely sophisticated autonomous navigation systems, allowing them to alter their mission specifications based upon the interpretations of the data they collect from the planetary systems that they are sent to explore.

As each sub-probe is released, it separates itself from its Communication Relay Pod, which remains within the flight trajectory of probe Evad, while the sub-probe itself proceeds on its way to its programmed destination. Subsequently, probe Evad's transmissions will consist of a random collection of reports as they are relayed by the Communication Relay Pods of the released sub-probes.

Behind the fabrication module is probe Evad's power module. The power module consists of an array of eight matter collectors that have the capability of collecting not only spatial debris, but spatial radiation as well. The three power processor sections of the power module system, convert the collected matter into energy that can then be repurposed back into whatever type of matter is required at any given time, whether into matter to be used to fabricate sub-probes, or into the compounds needed to create the fuel needed for probe Evad's ion-plasma propulsion system.

At the end of the craft resides probe Evad's ion-plasma propulsion system. The plan conceived by the DSEC entails a linear trajectory at a velocity never before even calculated by humankind. In fact, the final velocity agreed to by the majority of the members of the DSEC was one of the most debated issues regarding probe Evad's mission. Due to the preprogrammed gradual acceleration curve that was implemented at the time of probe Evad's launch, it would take 23 years for the ion-plasma propulsion system to accelerate probe Evad to its ultimate consistent cruising speed of just under ten times the speed of light, at which point, the deployment of sub-probes could commence.

As it had been only a few years since humankind had successfully developed a spacecraft capable of traveling at the speed of light, a rate of speed that had been believed for hundreds of years could not be achieved, many of the DSEC scientists at the time of probe Evad's launch believed that attaining the programmed velocity set for probe Evad, while justified in theory, was impossible and that probe Evad would break apart from the extreme gravitational forces and be destroyed prior to reaching its ultimate cruising velocity.

However, the majority of the DSEC scientists believed that due to the linear trajectory and the gradual staged increase in velocity the ion-plasma propulsion system would provide, probe Evad's structural integrity would continuously compensate for the gravitational forces until the programmed velocity was achieved, at which point the structural integrity of probe Evad would be stabilized and the fabrication module sub-probe release hatchway could safely be opened for the release of the sub-probes. As probe Evad would not be able to release sub-probes until it reached its cruising velocity and would only be able to communicate its progress via the Communication Relay Pods of the released sub-probes, it would take 23 years to confirm which group of scientists were correct.

It was, however, agreed to by every member of the DSEC, that probe Evad would be programmed with a linear trajectory and would utilize its sophisticated scanner array to search for points of interest, fabricate sub-probes specifically designed to investigate the destinations chosen by probe Evad's scanners and dispatch the sub-probes to investigate, when their release points were optimum for implementing a trajectory that would maximize the available power allocated to the sub-probe, as it was not possible to fabricate sub-probes large enough to equip them with long term power recharging capabilities like that of probe Evad.

It was also preprogrammed that the mission of the first sub-probe to be released would be to deploy the Mainframe Communication Relay Pod. The Mainframe Communication Relay Pod will be deployed with the pre-built Master-Server sub-probe.   The Master-Server sub-probe will remain attached to the Mainframe Communication Relay Pod, not only supplying it with additional power for transmission signal amplification, but, it will also house the Mini-Mainframe and short-term data storage units to be used to process the future deployed Communication Relay Pod's transmissions and their subsequent signal relays back to Earth.

Due to the complexity of the Master-Server sub-probe, as well as the sophistication of its programming, the Master-Server sub-probe was built simultaneously with probe Evad during the last eight years of probe Evad's construction at The DSEC Spaceport. The sophistication of its programming and the power capabilities to be provided by the Master-Server sub-probe's power module, also made fabricating the Master-Server sub-probe en route impossible. The Master-Server sub-probe was designed to exacting specifications to be the maximum size the fabrication module's deployment bay would allow for a sub-probe release. It has been calculated that the Master-Server sub-probe's power module will be capable of supplying the Mainframe Communication Relay

Pod with power for transmission signal relays for nearly 300 years.

Construction of probe Evad and the Master-Server sub-probe were completed within days of each other. Once construction was complete, it took just under two years for the DSEC scientists and construction engineers to complete all of the pre-launch programming and test sequences, which included the six months that was required to load the Master-Server sub-probe into probe Evad's fabrication module deployment bay and test its deployment, power-up sequence and subsequent activation of its communication sub-routines that would be required to initiate contact, link all deployed communications systems and begin the transmission relays.

A year after construction began on probe Evad, all of the remaining world governments that had a presence on the surface of the Moon, came to a unanimous agreement to also consolidate their efforts and resources that were dedicated to the Moon, towards developing and building a Transponder Array Complex (TAC) to be located on its surface. The agreed upon design of the array would consist of twelve huge satellite transponder dishes, positioned in a circular pattern a kilometer in diameter. Positioned in the precise center of the TAC, the domed Control and Earth Relay Complex (CERC) would be located.

The TAC and the CERC are engineering and construction marvels in their own rite. Due to the angle of probe Evad's linear trajectory relative to the Earth and the dynamics of the Moon's revolution around the Earth, the optimum positioning for the TAC to maintain the most consistent line-of-sight link with probe Evad, required that the TAC be located in one of the more mountainous regions of the Lunar surface, located in the northern hemisphere of the side of the Moon that faces the Earth. To date, the TAC, interconnected through the CERC, is the largest single complex ever constructed on the surface of the Moon.

Its design, development, construction and the powering-up of its systems took just over 34 years, of which, the first 14 years were primarily dedicated to clearing the terrain for the CERC, the Transponder Connection Platforms (TCP's) and the Transponder Power and Signal Transfer Conduits (TPSTC's), while simultaneously mining and processing the available helium-3 that would be used to fuel the CERC's fusion power reactor. Also, while mining the helium-3, huge storage and transfer facilities were constructed to store not only the processed helium-3, but also the water and oxygen generated as by-products from the helium-3 processing.

All of the major components of the TAC and all of its supporting structures were fabricated on Earth and/or at The DSEC Spaceport in low Earth orbit. As the completed components were either launched into Earth orbit or completed at the Spaceport, they were then loaded into one of the cargo transportation spacecrafts. A total of six cargo transportation spacecrafts were built to support the construction of the TAC; two were constantly in orbit around the Moon and two were constantly docked at The DSEC Spaceport, all being either loaded and/or unloaded, while one was en route to the Moon, the last was en route back to Earth. The construction of the TAC and the CERC, as well as all of its supporting structures and facilities, required a total of 73 enormous round-trip cargo transportation missions to the Moon.

Once the construction of the TAC and all of its supporting structures and facilities was complete, the six cargo transportation spacecrafts began being utilized to help facilitate the continued development of the Moon, as well as for transporting the helium-3 that continues to be mined in the Mare Tranquillitatis region of the Moon, back to Earth for use in the growing number of helium-3 fusion power reactors being built around the world. All of these fusion power reactors are being built based upon the reactor located in the LL 1 level of the CERC, which supplies the required power for the TAC, as well as, all of its supporting facilities.

The domed Control and Earth Relay Complex (CERC) consists of twelve main levels, two below ground level and ten above the surface. Positioned on the roof of the CERC is; the central, as well as the largest, transponder dish of the TAC, the Earth Satellite Relay Transponder Dish; used for relaying probe Evad's transmissions from the TAC to The DSEC Spaceport's UTD and the new updated Moon Traffic Control Communications Tower.

The following two pages contain the original rough drawing and floor plan assignments of the CERC, that were submitted by the DSEC Project Planning Council to the DSEC engineers, to be used as their guidelines for the formal development of the construction plans for the facility. These two pages are followed by general descriptions of all of the main departments that make up the levels of this extraordinary complex.

L 10: E.A.P.O.
Exterior Access Processing Operations

L 9: T.O.C. / M.T.C.
Transponder Operational Control and Moon Traffic Control

L 8: M.O.C.
Main Operational Control

L 7: P.S.&S. / F.S.
Personnel Support & Services and Food Services

L 6: T.P.Q / E.S. / R.P.Q. / P.C.S.
Temporary Personnel Quarters, Entertainment Services,
Resident Personnel Quarters and Personal Care Services

L 5: E.&A.C. / M.C. / R.L.
Exercise & Activity Center, Medical Center and Research Lab

L 4: L.O. / W.R. / G.S. / M.D. / R.P. / W.D.P.
Laundry Operations, Water Recycling, General Stores,
Medical Dispensary, Recycling Preparation and Waste
Disposal Preparation

L 3: H.&F.P. / F.&W.P
Hydroponics & Food Production and Food & Water Processing

L 2: M.C.O. / M.C.S.&D.P.
Master Computer Operations and Main Computer Storage & Data
Processing

L 1: T.P.O. / A.P.D.O.
Transponder Power Operations and Array Power Distribution
Operations

LL 1: A.G.E. / P.P. / W.P. / W.R.&D. / V.P.&S.
Artificial Gravity Enhancement, Power Production,
Water Production, Waste Recycling & Disposal and
Vehicle Preparation & Storage

LL 2: S.S. / F.M. / F.C. / I.O.P. / F.E. & E.P.
Supply Storage, Facility Maintenance, Fabrication Center,
In/Out Processing and Facility Entry & Exit Processing

The Original Rough Drawing and Floor Plan Assignments of the C.E.R.C.

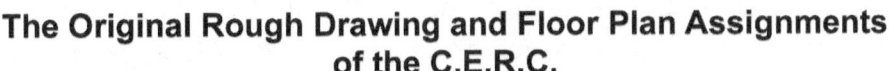

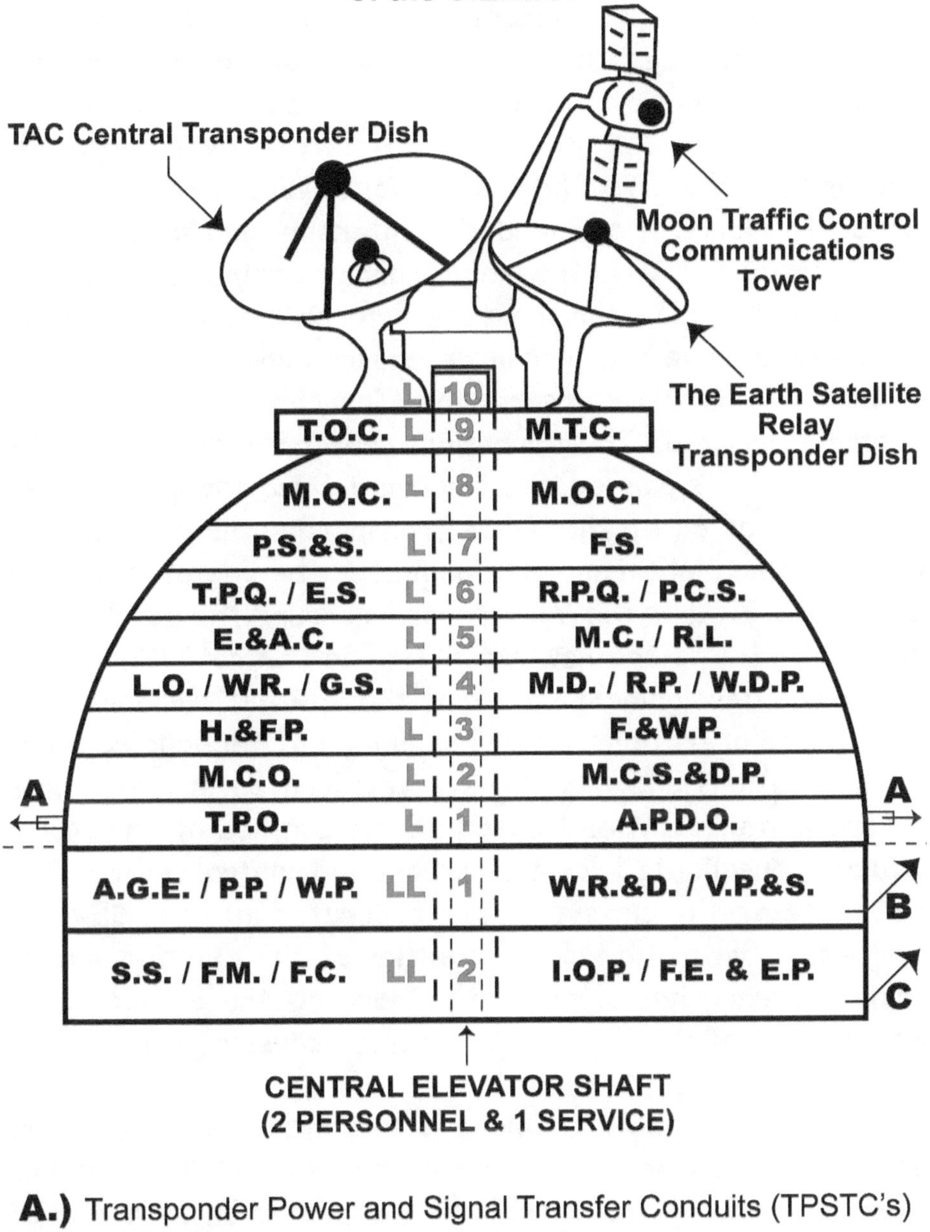

TAC Central Transponder Dish

Moon Traffic Control Communications Tower

The Earth Satellite Relay Transponder Dish

	L 10	
T.O.C.	L 9	M.T.C.
M.O.C.	L 8	M.O.C.
P.S.&S.	L 7	F.S.
T.P.Q. / E.S.	L 6	R.P.Q. / P.C.S.
E.&A.C.	L 5	M.C. / R.L.
L.O. / W.R. / G.S.	L 4	M.D. / R.P. / W.D.P.
H.&F.P.	L 3	F.&W.P.
M.C.O.	L 2	M.C.S.&D.P.
T.P.O.	L 1	A.P.D.O.
A.G.E. / P.P. / W.P.	LL 1	W.R.&D. / V.P.&S.
S.S. / F.M. / F.C.	LL 2	I.O.P. / F.E. & E.P.

A

A

B

C

**CENTRAL ELEVATOR SHAFT
(2 PERSONNEL & 1 SERVICE)**

A.) Transponder Power and Signal Transfer Conduits (TPSTC's)
B.) Lower Level 1 Access to the Lunar Surface
C.) Lower Level 2 Access to the Lunar Surface

Level 10 (L 10) is where the Exterior Access Processing Operations are located, which is where the CERC personnel are prepared with their spacesuits for exiting and re-entering the CERC through the rooftop pressurization chamber, accessing the roof of the CERC, allowing access to the central TAC transponder dish, the Earth Satellite Relay Transponder Dish and the Moon Traffic Control Communications Tower, for the performance of any needed maintenance and/or upgrades. Also located on L 10 is the maintenance machine room for the CERC's central elevator shafts, which contains two personnel elevators and the one main large service elevator.

Level 9 (L 9) is where the Transponder Operational Control is located. This operations center is where the TAC's control systems are located for maintaining the coordinated positioning of all of the TAC's transponder dishes, ensuring their continual optimum positioning for the line-of-sight link with probe Evad as the Moon revolves around the Earth. Also located on L 9 is the new Moon Traffic Control. During the design and development stages of the CERC, it was agreed to consolidate operations, as well as link all of the landing craft communications and tracking systems located in the various governmental facilities located on the surface of the Moon, into one consolidated communications and control center. The new state-of-the-art systems incorporated into the CERC, in conjunction with the linking together of the existing landing craft systems, has significantly improved the efficiency as well as the safety of the spacecrafts accessing the surface of the Moon.

Level 8 (L 8) is Main Operational Control, which consists of 341 workstations and small offices. While first-line monitoring and control operations are located on each level of the CERC with their respective equipment and systems, every operation of the TAC and the CERC are monitored and/or can be directly controlled from L 8. Of all the levels of the CERC, Main Operational Control has the largest, as well as, the most abundant number of windows of any of its levels. As L 8 is also where all senior operational supervisors are stationed, L 8 is where all personnel initially report immediately following facility in-processing, as well as, where all personnel must report prior to their final preparation for exiting the CERC.

Level 7 (L 7) is the location of Personnel Support & Services, as well as, Food Services. Along with all standard Human Resources related activities, Personnel Support & Services also provides personnel with private access to video teleconferencing for communicating with family and friends back on Earth. As all stations of the TAC and CERC are staffed with personnel around the clock, Food Services provides 24/7 access to a wide variety of daily prepared foods, as well as, a multitude of self-preparable food choices.

Level 6 (L 6) is the location of the Temporary Personnel Quarters, Entertainment Services, Resident Personnel Quarters and Personal Care Services. The Temporary Personnel Quarters are special personal quarters that were designed and built to accommodate the short-term visiting scientists and dignitaries. Entertainment Services is an off-duty area consisting of a variety of entertainment venues supporting both individual as well as group events. The Resident Personnel Quarters are the living quarters for the long-term stationed personnel. Intermingled with the Resident Personnel Quarters are the Personal Care Services consisting of private showers and bathing facilities, as well as, other general hygiene services including the resident barber and beautician.

Level 5 (L 5) is the location of the Exercise & Activity Center, the Medical Center and the Research Lab. While the CERC has artificial gravity enhancement, that very closely simulates the gravitational forces of Earth, the Exercise & Activity Center not only includes all of the equipment of a full-service gym, but also has highly specialized exercise equipment designed to help minimize the bone density loss inherent with traveling and working in low gravity. The Medical Center is a complete medical facility staffed 24/7 with a full compliment of specially trained nurses, doctors and surgeons. The Research Lab, staffed with many of Earth's leading scientific researchers, continues to study the origins of the Moon, as well as, the ongoing refinement of the helium-3 processing operations, towards ensuring the maximum possible yield of not only the helium-3, but also the critically needed water and oxygen by-products generated during the helium-3 mining process.

Level 4 (L 4) contains Laundry Operations, Water Recycling, General Stores, the Medical Dispensary, Recycling Preparation and Waste Disposal Preparation. Laundry Operations includes industrial sized washing machines for all general facility laundry services, such as for uniforms, towels and bed linens, as well as, a Laundromat for the Moon personnel's personal laundry purposes. The CERC's sophisticated Water Recycling operation reprocesses all of the water used throughout the facility, separating out any impurities and transfers both the re-purified water, as well as, all liquid waste to Lower Level 1 (LL 1) for final processing. The General Stores and the Medical Dispensary are staffed 24/7 providing access to not only the TAC and the CERC personnel, but to all the personnel stationed on the Moon, to general personal products and supplies, as well as, any needed medications. The Recycling Preparation and Waste Disposal Preparation operations are the personnel drop off locations and the preprocessing operations for all personal, as well as, facility operations solid waste. These two operations perform the separation and preparation of all facility solid waste materials before transferring the waste via the CERC's large central service elevator to Lower Level 1 (LL 1) for final processing and disposal.

Level 3 (L 3) is the location of Hydroponics & Food Production and Food & Water Processing. The efficiency and productivity of Hydroponics & Food Production and the Food & Water

Processing operations have not only surpassed the demand for food by the CERC personnel, but, have surpassed the demand for food by all of the personnel currently stationed on the Moon. As the CERC's food production currently surpasses the amount of food required to support the personnel stationed on the Moon, the food-related supplies that are part of the regular cargo transportation re-supply missions from Earth are primarily specialty-ordered food items and fresh water to help supplement the water being produced at the CERC and from the helium-3 mining process. While the research being performed at the Research Lab on Level 5 (L 5), as well as, back on Earth, continues to help with the steadily increasing volume of water being produced on the Moon, the amount of water being produced is still falling short of the demand imposed by the number of people currently stationed on the Moon, subsequently, substantial fresh water shipments are still required from Earth.

Level 2 (L 2) consists of Master Computer Operations and Main Computer Storage & Data Processing. There are computer terminals and personal computers throughout the TAC and the CERC, however, L 2 is the location of the mass-storage memory modules, the mainframe data processing CPU's and retrieval systems and the operational master computational servers. While all operational computational functions and special task requests are initiated and monitored from Main Operational Control on Level 8 (L 8), all first-line monitoring and physical continual computer system maintenance is performed on L 2. Along with supporting all of the computing needs of the TAC and the CERC, sufficient computing power has been installed to also decompress the incoming transmissions received from probe Evad, as well as, process and recompress them for their relay transmission to The DSEC Spaceport's UTD, and subsequently, back to Earth.

Level 1 (L 1) is the location of the Transponder Power Operations and the Array Power Distribution Operations.

Located at ground level, extending outwardly from the CERC in a circular 30° spread pattern, like that of the twelve analog clock positions, are the twelve Transponder Power and Signal Transfer Conduits (TPSTC's). The twelve TPSTC's are each connected to their respective Transponder Connection Platforms (TCP's). Installed on top of each of the TCP's are the twelve main Transponder Dishes that make up the outer ring of the Transponder Array. Each of the Transponder Dishes is located .5 kilometers from the Central Power Distribution Module of the CERC, which are connected to the array via the TCP's and are linked to the CERC and the central TAC Transponder Dish via the TPSTC's, which makes the TAC a full kilometer in diameter, making the TAC not only the largest single complex ever constructed on the surface of the Moon, but, also the largest Virtual Transponder Dish ever constructed by humankind. To expedite the rotation of personnel between the CERC and the TCP's, each of the TPSTC's contains a dedicated Monorail Transport Vehicle (MTV) capable of seating six personnel, the standard number of personnel, per TCP, per shift. If needed, cargo transport units can be added and connected to the MTV's for the movement of equipment and/or replacement parts required in the TCP's or for the Transponder Dishes. The TPSTC's and the TCP's are pressurized and supported with breathable air, so spacesuits are not required in these areas of the TAC, however, they are not supported with any gravity enhancement, so, personnel must either wear the enhanced weighted artificial gravity belts and boots, or operate under the low gravity conditions while in these areas.

Lower Level 1 (LL 1), the first level of the CERC located below ground level, is the location of; Artificial Gravity Enhancement, Power Production, Water Production, Waste Recycling & Disposal and Vehicle Preparation & Storage. Living and working in low gravity conditions had long been a major obstacle to humankind with regard to space exploration.

Great strides had been made with artificial gravity generation aboard spacecrafts and orbiting space stations, however, it wasn't until the development and construction of the CERC that artificial gravity was achieved on the surface of the Moon and construction is now underway towards its integration into the International Research Facility on the surface of the planet Mars. Due to the size of the equipment and the nature of the operations located on these levels, the ceiling heights of the two lower levels of the CERC are nearly twice the height of the other levels, with the exception of Main Operational Control on L 8, which also has a tall ceiling height due to its large observational windows and the huge structural support arches for supporting the enormous weight of L 9, as well as, the central transponder dish of the TAC, the Earth Satellite Relay Transponder Dish and the Moon Traffic Control Communications Tower that are all located on the roof of the CERC. The Artificial Gravity Enhancement operations consists of the electromagnetic field generator, its sophisticated computer monitoring systems, the system's main field transfer node and main transfer conduit that runs up through the CERC in tandem with the facility's elevator shafts. Branching off of the main transfer conduit and incorporated into every floor of the CERC, is the network of electromagnetic transfer coils that generate the facility's artificial gravity, which functions in conjunction with the specially designed lightweight belts and boots worn by the CERC personnel. Power Production is the helium-3 fueled fusion reactor. The helium-3 is transferred from the huge external storage tanks, where the helium-3 is stored during the mining and processing operations, via a highly pressurized underground pipeline directly to the fusion reactor. The CERC's fusion reactor generates sufficient power to not only power all of the TAC and CERC's systems, but will also provide sufficient power to meet all of the power requirements of the new Personnel Housing Complex (PHC) currently under construction. The new PHC is scheduled to be completed within the next few years and will be capable of supporting 1,400 personnel when fully operational. Water Production first purifies the water generated as a by-product from the helium-3 mining process, which is also transferred via an underground pipeline that runs in tandem with the helium-3 supply pipeline and delivers the externally stored water directly to Water Production operations. When the initial stage of testing and water purification is complete, water from the L 4 Water Recycling operations is added and the mixture undergoes another round of purification and chlorination. When this stage is complete, fresh water from the supply shipments sent from Earth is added and this final water mixture is then pumped to the Water Processing operations on L 3 where fluorination and final testing is performed. When the final testing is complete, the approved water is then pumped and disseminated to the multitude of water dispensing stations throughout the CERC. Waste Recycling & Disposal operations processes the solid and liquid wastes that are separated and prepared on L 4. Any of the waste that can be repurposed, such as most of the paper and plastic materials, are shredded and/or reground and are transferred directly to the raw material holding compartments located one level below in the Fabrication Center on LL 2. Any of the waste that cannot be repurposed somehow in the Fabrication Center is then prepared for disposal. The solid waste is compacted into cubes measuring ten feet per side and wrapped in a specially formulated wrapping film made from a combination of the recycled paper and plastics. The solid waste cubes are then transferred to Vehicle Preparation where they are loaded onto the specially designed transport carts and prepared for transport to the external staging area, where they are unloaded and await removal from the surface of the Moon. As the cargo transportation spacecrafts arrive from Earth and the Lunar Delivery crafts deliver the various personnel and supplies to the surface of the Moon, when all of their supplies are unloaded, the solid waste cubes are then loaded and transferred to the cargo transportation spacecrafts for their return to Earth, where they are utilized as fuel in the zero-emission solid waste Power Plants, that burn solid wastes at extremely high temperatures, yet generate no air or water pollution during their electricity generation process. The liquid waste, is transferred into cubical containers, also made from the recycled paper and plastics, identical in size to the solid waste cubes, however, they are also coated both externally as well as internally with a specially formulated heat resistant plastic resin, which is also reinforced with Lunar rock dust ensuring they maintain their structural integrity during transport and deployment. As with the solid waste cubes, when the liquid waste containers are full, they are also transferred to Vehicle Preparation where they are loaded onto the specially designed transport carts and prepared for transport to the external staging area, where they too are unloaded and await removal from the surface of the Moon. Along with the solid waste cubes, the liquid waste containers are transferred via the Lunar Delivery crafts to the cargo transportation spacecrafts; however, the liquid waste containers are not returned to Earth. Once the containers are loaded on board the cargo transportation spacecrafts, small directional thruster engine modules are attached to the containers and they are then moved to the deployment staging area. En route back to Earth, once the cargo transportation spacecraft has reached its consistent velocity, the liquid waste containers are deployed and their thruster engines are engaged, setting them on a collision course with the Sun. Once the containers cross the orbital path of the planet Mercury, the gravitational forces of the Sun exponentially increases the speed of the containers until they arrive at the distance from the Sun where the temperature reaches the point that vaporizes the container and its contents. Vehicle

Preparation & Storage is not only where the solid and liquid waste containers are loaded onto the transport carts and prepared for transport to the external staging area, but is also where maintenance is performed on all of the TAC and the CERC vehicles. This is also where all personnel transport vehicles are recharged and stored when not in use. Vehicles have access to the Lunar surface and enter and exit the CERC via the large LL 1 underground pressurization chamber. For expediting the entry and exit of personnel only, there is also a smaller secondary pressurization chamber, which is large enough for six personnel per pressurization cycle.

Lower Level 2 (LL 2), the lowermost level of the CERC, is the location of Supply Storage, Facility Maintenance, the Fabrication Center, In/Out Processing and Facility Entry & Exit Processing. Supply Storage is where all personnel consumable supplies, such as specialty-ordered food and drinks, personal hygiene supplies, General Stores inventory and Medical supplies are stored. This is also where all general facility support materials are stored such as clothing, spacesuit components, linens and personal cleaning supplies. All equipment and/or raw material supplies are stored in Facility Maintenance, the Fabrication Center, or the external staging area. Facility Maintenance is the centralized location for all general facility maintenance tools and equipment, as well as, where all small equipment repair is performed. It is also where all of the general facility consumables are stored, such as light bulbs, air filters, general facility cleaning supplies and etc. The Fabrication Center is where the processed recycled paper and plastics are staged in the raw material holding compartments. The Fabrication Center is where the wrapping film used to wrap the solid waste cubes is manufactured and stored, as well as, where the liquid waste container cubes are made. The Fabrication Center also includes a complete machine shop capable of manufacturing most general facility and vehicle replacement parts. In/Out Processing is the personnel administration office where all personnel are processed upon entering and exiting the CERC. Upon entering the CERC all personnel documentation and orders are confirmed, identification badges are issued and the embedded biometric and location access chips are programmed and activated, Temporary or Resident Personnel Quarters located on L 6 are assigned dependent upon the individual personnel's visitation duration, the designated command supervisor is advised of the personnel arrival, the personnel are provided with the CERC Personnel Handbook and Resident Informational Documentation and they are instructed where and to whom to report to in Main Operational Control on L 8, which is where all personnel must immediately report upon completion of In-Processing. In preparation to exit the CERC all personnel first pass through In/Out Processing. All orders and purpose for exiting the CERC are confirmed with the exiting personnel's designated command supervisor and Facility Entry & Exit Processing is advised so that the required spacesuit and any needed equipment can be prepared. If the personnel are exiting the CERC due to the end of their visitation and are returning to Earth, or are preparing to leave for the International Research Facility on the surface of the planet Mars, their identification badges are collected, all location access is deactivated and Facility Maintenance is advised so that the Personnel Quarters that they were assigned can be cleaned, powered-down and returned to ready-status for new personnel arrival. Facility Entry & Exit Processing is where all activities related to physically entering and exiting the CERC from the surface of the Moon take place. Here, all personnel are assisted with their spacesuit and operational reviews are performed for any utilized equipment. While LL 2 has duplicative pressurization chambers to those located on LL 1, one large chamber for vehicle access to the Lunar surface and one smaller secondary pressurization chamber, which is large enough for six personnel per pressurization cycle, each Level is designated primary purposes. The large chamber on LL 1 is primarily for usage by the personnel transport vehicles, the Lunar exploratory vehicles and the Waste Disposal transport vehicles and the smaller secondary chamber is primarily for usage by the general incoming and outgoing CERC personnel. The large chamber on LL 2 is primarily for usage by the Supply Storage transport vehicles and the TAC and the CERC Facility Maintenance vehicles and the smaller secondary chamber is primarily for usage by the Supply Storage and Facility Maintenance personnel. As there is no central elevator access to Vehicle Preparation & Storage, which is where the external access pressurization chambers are located on LL 1, there is a personnel lift platform that travels only between LL 1 and LL 2 for the movement of personnel between Vehicle Preparation & Storage and Facility Entry & Exit Processing, which is large enough to hold six personnel in full spacesuits. There is also no access to any of the other operations on LL 1 from Vehicle Preparation & Storage, as all personnel must be processed through Facility Entry & Exit Processing and can only enter and/or exit the CERC through In/Out Processing, which are both located on LL 2.

Since the completion of the TAC and the CERC, primary construction focus on the surface of the Moon has been dedicated to the Personnel Housing Complex (PHC), the enormous residential facility which is urgently needed to help support the rapid Moon-based population growth.

On this 43rd anniversary of the formation of the DSEC, the date that coincides with probe Evad's scheduled release of the Master-Server sub-probe and activation sequence initiation of the Mainframe Communication Relay Pod, the DSEC Mission Control Center on Earth is occupied to capacity with DSEC scientists and construction engineers. The DSEC Spaceport's UTD has been successfully linked to the Earth Satellite Relay Transponder Dish located on the roof of the CERC, which is located at the precise center of the TAC constructed on the surface of the Moon and the full bandwidth of the array has been focused on the trajectory of probe Evad, awaiting the deployment and activation sequence initiation confirmation from the Mainframe Communication Relay Pod.

In a moment in humankind's history, witnessed by millions of people throughout the world, those in the DSEC Mission Control Center, those stationed at The DSEC Spaceport and those stationed at the TAC and the CERC on the surface of Moon, the main communication display screens located in all of the respective DSEC Master Control Rooms lit up with the activation sequence data stream being received from the Mainframe Communication Relay Pod - the thunderous uproar and applause in each of the DSEC Master Control Rooms was close to deafening. One hundred and forty-three minutes after the activation sequence data stream began; the first transmission from the Mainframe Communication Relay Pod was initiated.

This first transmission included component readouts from all of probe Evad's operational systems as well as the first photographic images, images of probe Evad taken during the deployment of the Master-Server sub-probe. The images showed that probe Evad had indeed survived, without any apparent structural damage, the acceleration to is cruising velocity. The component readouts also indicated that probe Evad had somehow exceeded its programmed velocity and has reached and is maintaining a velocity of exactly 10 times the speed of light. DSEC mission supervisors continue to examine the compiled data in the attempt to determine how this was achieved, as the final calculations and programming simulations performed at the time of probe Evad's launch, indicated that the maximum light speed velocity achievable would fall just short of the 10 times exponential.

As probe Evad is traveling at such an accelerated velocity and its fabrication module is capable of nearly instantaneous fabrication of sub-probes, due to the fact that probe Evad will autonomously select points of interest in which to explore, as well as designate the mission directives of the released sub-probes and the Mainframe Communication Relay Pod will only relay transmissions when its data stream buffer is full, in order to maximize the usage of its finite power supply, it is unknown as to when subsequent transmissions will be received – only that each transmission will be a random collection of transmissions relayed by the sub-probes probe Evad has dispatched.

With the focus of the TAC located on the surface of the Moon now dedicated to the trajectory of probe Evad, all of the DSEC personnel, along with all of humanity, await the subsequent Mainframe Communication Relay Pod's transmissions with great expectations...

Loading Transmission: 06 . 21 . 07 . 01 . 20...

.01
The Blue Plasma Fires Of Whiteroc

It was the brilliant shimmering blue color that first attracted probe Evad's long-range scanners to this world. However, when it was first detected, its distance from probe Evad made it impossible to determine if the shimmering blue color was oceanic, or atmospheric activity – a Level 3 sub-probe was fabricated and launched.

Upon entering initial scanner range of the planet, the sub-probe activated its topographical scanners and detected that the shimmering blue color was neither oceanic nor atmospheric, but was instead, the movement of blue plasma fires across the planet's surface, which encompasses the entire planet. While the sub-probe collected, compiled and evaluated the statistical data regarding the plasma fires, the bio-life scanners were unable to acquire clear consistent readings from the planet's surface; however, an enormous amount of bio-activity was detected in orbit around the planet.

When the sub-probe reached full scanner capable range, it activated its first contact observational protocols and engaged its propulsion system to de-accelerate to its all-stop initial observational satellite position. When the sub-probe achieved its all-stop positioning, its remaining onboard scanners were activated.

The bio-life scanners found obvious intelligent life, as there is a great deal of spacecraft activity interacting with a multitude of satellite space stations that are in orbit around the planet. The physical appearance of the inhabitants of this world are as of yet unknown, as no observations of them have been recorded by the sub-probe thus far. All activity observed thus far, has been that of the spacecrafts docking and undocking with the satellite space stations, with occasional crafts leaving and entering the planet's orbit - the destination and/or origin of the spacecrafts leaving and arriving at the planet have not yet been tracked. Due to the blue plasma fires on the planet's surface, there has been no bio-activity of any kind detected physically on the planet's surface, however, observations thus far clearly indicate that an intricate underground network of structures are in existence. As of yet, due to the interference caused by the blue plasma fires, in combination with the bio-electrical fields being dispersed in between the satellite space stations and the apparent underground cities, the actual size of the structures, or how deeply the structures are built into the planet's surface, are currently unknown.

The sub-probe's onboard linguistic compilers have completed their initial evaluation of this world's language structure based upon the intercepted communication transmissions between the orbiting space stations, the spacecrafts and the underground network of cities. Based upon this initial evaluation and the language structure model that has been compiled, the closest English translation of the name that appears to have been given to this world by its inhabitants is Whiteroc.

The inhabitants of the planet Whiteroc have developed construction materials capable of withstanding the extreme temperatures and susceptible flammability of the blue plasma fires that rampage the planet's surface. The only means of entry into the massive structures of the Whiteroc Cities is through the utilization of the molecular decomposition and re-composition portal technology linked to the space stations in orbit around the planet. The inhabitants of the planet also developed the portal technology.

The inhabitants of Whiteroc are apparently unaware of the existence of the sub-probe as no attempts of communication, or contact, has been initiated by them thus far. The sub-probe will continue its observations of Whiteroc from its current observational satellite position and will temporarily suspend any attempt at first contact until more data can be collected and determinations made as to the purpose of the orbiting satellite space stations, the functions of the interacting spacecrafts and more is learned and understood about the inhabitants and their purpose for inhabiting such a seemingly inhospitable world.

.02
Rainbow Island City

The surface of the sixth planet in the Artaigra 2.2 System is completely covered with liquid almost identical to that of the water located on planet Earth, except for one small landmass, which is completely covered with interconnecting structures that reach a height of just over 2 kilometers from the water's surface. The inhabitants have named their world, Rainbow Island City, after the brilliant perpetual rainbow that shines on the planets horizon.

Probe Evad launched a Level 2 sub-probe to investigate this planet when its long-range scanners detected the existence of what was anticipated to be liquid water. When the sub-probe reached its full scanner capable range, activated its first contact observational protocols and engaged its propulsion system to de-accelerate to its all-stop initial observational satellite position, its topographical scanners confirmed that the liquid on the planet's surface was indeed almost identical to the water located on planet Earth, with the exception of the existence of two as of yet unidentifiable chemical components.

When the sub-probe achieved its all-stop positioning and activated the remainder of its onboard scanners, the bio-life scanners were unable to detect any known life forms on, or in, the liquid on the planet's surface. While evaluating what was initially believed to be a completely liquid surface, the bio-life scanners detected an isolated dense concentration of bio-activity. The sub-probe refocused its topographical scanners to the location of the bio-activity and discovered the only confirmed landmass on the planet's surface. Due to the dense concentration of the bio-activity, it was not possible for the sub-probe to determine the precise number of inhabitants that occupy the interconnected structures built upon the landmass. While focusing the bio-scanners on the structures, two spacecrafts were detected emerging from the liquid surface approximately .25 kilometers from the landmass at an astonishing velocity.

Within four Earth hours the two crafts had reached a distance of one thousand kilometers from the sub-probe, at which point they came to an abrupt instantaneous stop. Seconds after they arrived, a bio-electrical transmission field was detected emanating from both crafts directed at the sub-probe. At that moment, the planet became no longer visible to any of the sub-probe's onboard scanners. The sub-probe immediately activated its first contact communication protocols and began transmitting its data stream of mission greetings and language structure information packets.

Shortly after the sub-probe's language data streams began, the crafts began returning a communication stream built upon the sub-probe's core binary mathematical system. Translation of the crafts initial data streams included little information beyond the name the inhabitants have given their world. The majority of the crafts communication streams were requests for detailed information regarding the origin of the sub-probe and purpose for its proximity to their world.

Due to the interference from the bio-electrical fields being generated by the crafts, along with the repetition of their communication data streams, the sub-probe has been unable to determine the number of occupants, if any, aboard the crafts, nor has it been able to reestablish any scanner acquisition of the planet. The craft's transmissions do however clearly indicate that the inhabitants of this world carefully guard their existence and will no longer allow the sub-probe to observe their world until all of the sub-probe's systems and mission objectives are clearly understood. The sub-probe continues to send its first contact mission greetings, as well as, has begun transmitting all of the available onboard info-packets regarding the mission objectives of probe Evad and the long-range scanner report that initiated the fabrication and deployment of this sub-probe. However, as per the first contact communication protocols, the sub-probe will not transmit any of the onboard info-packets regarding its, or probe Evad's, trajectory or Earth origin, until more is known and understood about the inhabitants of this world and their alien species interactive directives – during this exchange, the sub-probe will maintain a peaceful communication posture.

Due to the limited number of scans that were completed prior to them being blocked by the two spacecrafts, thus far, other than the name the inhabitants have given to this world, the height of the structures built on the one and only detected landmass on the planet's surface and the fact that this world is indeed inhabited by some form of intelligent life, little is known about this world.

The liquid surface is extremely calm with only subtle ripples, with no detectable waves and as initially reported;

the bio-scanners were unable to detect any life forms on the surface of, or within the liquid itself. The atmosphere is extremely thin, with a high concentration of hydrogen and slow moving clouds, but the initial atmospheric scans indicated little to no detectable weather pattern activity. Insufficient scans were completed in order to determine the molecular composition of the materials used to construct the discovered interconnected structures, how they were constructed or whether the materials used are native to this world. As of yet, no physical observance of the inhabitants of this world has been made, nor was sufficient information acquired in order to estimate the total number of inhabitants. The sub-probes efforts towards a peaceful open information exchange will continue.

Snow Cloud Rock Range

Planet Debta 20 of the Konetar System is a frozen world covered in an estimated 4.3 kilometers of snow and ice. The only non-snow-covered land is a gray rock mountain range that encompasses the planets' surface around its equator and is just under 162 kilometers in width at its widest point. The speculation is that the gravitational forces caused by the extreme rate of the planets' rotation are forming the mountain range.

Probe Evad has discovered that The Konetar System, once believed to contain many stars and subsequently, potentially a multitude of planets, in fact, contains only one massive star with a single orbiting planet. The single planet, named Debta 20 by the human scientist that first discovered it, has long been a mystery, as it seemingly maintained a rapid orbit around the system's center, but, due to the system's distance from Earth, as well as, the bright glow of the system's orbital plane, its parent star could never be identified. Probe Evad has now discovered that Debta 20 is indeed, the only planet of this system and the glow at the system's center is not a collection of stars, but, is instead, a single massive star – a Level 1 sub-probe was fabricated and deployed to investigate this system further.

As the sub-probe approached the Konetar System, its long-range scanners confirmed that the glow of the orbital disc of this system, was not only a single planet, but also contained millions of asteroids, most no larger than one meter in diameter, all in a singular plane orbit around the massive central star. The sub-probe's initial long-range scans indicate that this central star is just over 1,000 times the diameter of the Sun of planet Earth's solar system. These scans establish the Konetar Star as one of the largest known stars documented to date. Planet Debta 20 is approximately 431 times the size of planet Earth and rotates on its axis at an astonishing rate of speed, completing a single rotation in just 14 Earth hours. Along with its rapid rotation, Debta 20 also orbits the massive central star in just 286 Earth days. The gravitational forces generated by the combination of Debta 20's rapid rotation and expeditious orbit around the Konetar Star draws the asteroids through the orbital plane like a huge trailing tail.

It is as of yet unknown whether the asteroid field is the result of orbital debris that failed to coalesce during the formation of Debta 20, the result of one or more planetary collisions, or ejecta from Debta 20 itself. As initially reported, it is speculated that the mountain range that encircles Debta 20 along its equator, is being formed by the extreme gravitational forces caused by the planet's rapid rotation. Multiple instances of planetary debris have been observed being ejected into space from the mountain range of the planet's surface, which has lead to the speculation that the Konetar system's asteroid field is being created by a process of the gradual self-destruction of Debta 20. The mountain range that encircles the planet is the longest contiguous mountain range ever documented and the only known mountain range to encircle an entire planet. Also as initially reported, the mountain range of Debta 20 is the only non-snow-covered land on the planet's surface. Debta 20 orbits the Konetar Star at a distance of nearly twice that of the planet Uranus of Earth's solar system and even though the Konetar Star is over 1,000 times the diameter of the Earth's Sun, the sub-probe's long-range scanners indicate that its temperature output is thousand's of degrees less. Subsequently, the combination of the distance from its star and the surface wind speeds that are generated by the planet's rapid rotation, the extremely cold conditions have left the remaining surface of Debta 20 a desolate frozen expanse of snow and ice estimated to be 4.3 kilometers thick.

Due to the unexpected extreme density of the asteroid field of the Konetar System and the limited maneuverability of the Level 1 sub-probe, the sub-probe has positioned itself in a synchronous orbit with Debta 20 just outside of the Konetar System's orbital debris plane. As at this distance from Debta 20 the sub-probe will be unable to utilize the planet's gravity to maintain the selected observational orbit, it will exhaust its onboard power systems very rapidly. Probe Evad has launched a Level 3 sub-probe to replace this sub-probe for the continued observation of this system.

.04
Water Rock Sculpture

Probe Evad's long-range scanners detected liquid water on this planet, the eighth planet of fourteen, of this binary star system and deployed a Level 3 sub-probe to investigate. As the sub-probe approached this system, its long-range scanners documented the binary stars to be a pair of White Dwarfs at opposite ends of their color spectrums, one at its peak hot-white stage, with the other at its near death cool-red stage. The two stars are at a surprisingly close proximity to one another with their closest orbital crossing placing them just over 43 million miles apart. This close proximity of these two Dwarf Stars is generating extremely strong, varying gravitational fields, which has placed each of the fourteen planets of this system in their own unique orbital plane.

Also, upon entering initial scanner range of the planet, the sub-probe activated its topographical scanners and confirmed that the liquid water on the planet's surface is almost identical, in both composition, as well as, temperature ranges, to the water on planet Earth, with the slight difference being that the water of this world contains just a slightly higher mineral content. However, while similar in composition and temperature to the water of planet Earth, the volume of water on the surface of this world is slightly less than half the volume of the water found on planet Earth. The long-range scans also documented that this world is also similar to planet Earth in that it is just 3,410 kilometers larger in diameter and rotates once on its axis in 28.6 hours. The one major planetary difference between this world and planet Earth is, due to this world's distance from its system's central binary stars, it takes the equivalent of 1,144 Earth days for this world to complete a single orbit.

When the sub-probe reached full scanner capable range, activated its first contact observational protocols and achieved its all-stop observational satellite positioning, upon activating the remainder of its onboard scanners, no orbital satellite or spacecraft activity was detected in orbit around this world or within this planetary system. Bio-life scans have documented an upright-walking tri-pedal species with four upper-body appendages, along with a multitude of apparent subordinate animal species on the planet's surface.

The sub-probe's onboard linguistic compilers have completed their initial evaluation of this world's extremely basic language structure based upon the intercepted primitive radio-signal-based surface transmissions. All indications are that the species that inhabit this world are unaware of life in the Universe outside of that of their own world. The identified name the dominant tri-pedal species have given to their world is Gollredd.

Located in the largest ocean of the planet Gollredd is a mountain that the planet's scientists speculate was carved out by the glacier fields and mineral-heavy flash floods that occurred during the planet's formation. The mountain's summit is also noticeably the planet's highest elevation, as it is nearly twice the elevation of any other location on the planet. The closest English translation of the name given to this mountain by the inhabitants of the planet is Water Rock Sculpture.

Surface scans have found little to no major industry on the surface of the planet. The only major technical achievement observed thus far is, the multitude of radio-signal-based transceivers that encompass much of the planet. The only forms of transportation observed thus far is limited to the surface of the planet, in fact, no airborne activity whatsoever has been observed thus far, including no flight-capable life forms. The main form of surface transportation is animal-drawn, four-wheeled open carriages of various sizes. The carriages are drawn by animals similar in size to the elephants found on planet Earth. Their physical appearance however, is much different in that they have and walk upon six appendages, have long thin necks and very small heads with no apparent eyes. These animals are attached to the carriages by straps that are connected to harnesses that are wrapped around their main body. A collar worn around their neck is attached to straps, that run through eyelets of the harness and the ends are held by the drivers of the carriages. The animals are controlled through a series of vocal commands and by the straps held by the carriage drivers.

Transportation across the liquid water expanses appears to be limited to the surface via small manually powered crafts built from the trees that line the coastlines of the planet's landmasses. A multitude of life forms have been documented in the water, however, little to no interaction has been observed thus far between them and those that inhabit the planet's surface. In fact, thus far, the surface-based life forms have not been observed physically entering the liquid water and none of the water-based life forms have been observed leaving the water to come on to the planet's surface.

No organized agriculture has been observed. The main source of food consumed by the inhabitants of the planet consists of fruit-like items that grow naturally on the abundant trees and plants located on the surface of the planet. The inhabitants pick and immediately eat the various food items as is, with no observed forms of preparation. There have also been no observations of any liquid consumption by the inhabitants. It is speculated that the fluid requirements of the inhabitants of the planet are met solely through their food consumption.

Other than the activities of those that have been identified as the scientists of this world, there appears to be no noticeable difference in the activities of the inhabitants and no forms of organized labor or commerce has been observed. There has also been no clear indication of gender within the tri-pedal species and the manner in which their species is propagated is as of yet unknown.

As all indications from the observations made thus far are that the intelligent inhabitants of this world are extremely primitive and as initially reported, based upon the evaluation of the intercepted transmissions taking place on the planet's surface, as it appears the inhabitants are unaware of life outside of that of their own world, the sub-probe will remain in its current satellite observational location and will continue to observe this world, however, no attempt to communicate with any of the life forms of this world will be made at this time.

.05
The Dusk Fires Of Teroknor

As the sub-probe in orbit around the planet Gollredd repositioned itself to observe the dark side of the planet in order to document the nocturnal activities of the planet's inhabitants, a large number of transmissions were intercepted containing references to an upcoming event in the night skies. The closest English translation of the event is "red tremor Teroknor". After documenting a multitude of references to Teroknor and the descriptions of the upcoming event, it became clear that the event was in reference to one of this system's outer planets. As initially reported, due to the close proximity of the two Dwarf Stars to each other located at the center of this planetary system, extremely strong, varying gravitational fields has placed each of the fourteen planets of this system in their own unique orbital plane. The sub-probe has reloaded its original long-range scans of this system into its onboard planetary system simulator and has run extended modeling of the orbital cycles of all of the planets in this system.

The results of the simulation indicate that the orbital path of the ninth planet of this system will bring the ninth planet within 429,000 kilometers of the orbital path of Gollredd. Due to the varying angles of the orbital planes of the two planets and the speed in which both planets orbit the central Dwarf Stars, the ninth planet, named Teroknor by the inhabitants of the planet Gollredd, will cross Gollredd's night skies during the planet's current orbital cycle. It has been calculated that the orbital planes of Gollredd and Teroknor run at a near perfect 90° to one another. The diameter of Teroknor is approximately 1/3 that of Gollredd. Due to the combination of Teroknor's size and its distance from Gollredd, Teroknor will appear in Gollredd's night sky very similar in size as the Moon appears to the inhabitants of planet Earth. It has been calculated that this crossing and the appearance of Teroknor in Gollredd's night sky will last for a total of just over six Gollredd rotations and will include a full eclipse of Teroknor as Gollredd passes between it and the two Dwarf Stars. The sub-probe's long-range scanners located the current position of Teroknor and the sub-probe set course to orbit Teroknor for closer observation.

Upon establishing orbit of Teroknor, the sub-probe performed its entire initial topographical and bio-life scans of the planet. The scans found no form of industrial or technological development on the surface whatsoever. The bio-life scanners have thus far only located and documented quad-pedal life forms located on several of the landmasses located within the equatorial region of the planet. The documented life forms are physiologically similar to the reptiles found on planet Earth. The majority of the life forms documented thus far are similar in size and stature to that of the deer and moose found on planet Earth, although, two species have been documented that are equivalent to that of planet Earth's rodents. The sub-probe's onboard linguistic compilers have thus far been unable to establish any form of structured communications between the inhabitants of Teroknor. All of the documented interactions between the species thus far have been a series of general vocally generated sounds. The only physical interactions between the species observed thus far have been that of peaceful coexistence. Other than size, there appears to be no one dominant species, nor have any form of predator/prey interrelations been observed. The topographical scanners have found no indications of any form of organized agriculture and all of the documented species independently feed on the various vegetation of the planet's surface. There is an extremely low volume of liquid water on the surface of the planet; however, the atmospheric scanners have documented very high moisture concentrations in the clouds, also primarily located in the equatorial regions of the planet.

The entire northern landmass of the planet Teroknor is plagued by molten rock fires ignited by the change in atmospheric temperature that occurs each day during the landmass's dusk. The fires are extinguished each day by the extreme winds and rapid temperature drop that occurs during the landmass's daily dawn, leaving the surface of the landmass a charred, uninhabitable expanse. Due to this weather phenomenon, Teroknor is the only known planet whose surface temperature is consistently hotter on its dark side.

It is speculated that due to the cycle of the molten rock fires and the unusual surface wind patterns that are generated by them, even with Teroknor's extreme distance from this systems central Dwarf Stars, this cycle of fires maintains the planet's surface temperature sufficient to sustain the quad-pedal species of the equatorial region. The atmospheric scans have documented that the extreme heat generated by the night cycle of molten rock fires rapidly evaporates the liquid water on the surface of the planet. The combination of the rising heat with the rapid rotation of the planet generates unusual wind patterns that not only extinguishes the fires on the daylight-side of the planet during its daily dawn cycle, but also pushes the rising moisture from the liquid water evaporation towards the equatorial region of the planet. This cycle also causes the moisture to build so rapidly in the equatorial region, that by mid-day, a cycle equal to five Earth hours of torrential rainfall takes place, which leads to a drinking frenzy by all of the planet's life forms.

Upon completion of all of the initial bio-life and topographical scans, the sub-probe set course back to Gollredd, placing itself outside of the planet's gravity well in a geostationary orbit above the northern polar region of the planet for optimal viewing of the planetary crossing of these two worlds. The extended modeling of the orbital cycles of all of the planets in this system that was generated by the sub-probe's onboard planetary system simulator indicates that the planetary crossing of these two worlds takes place the equivalent of once every 13 Earth years. The gravitational stress this crossing will have on both worlds is currently incalculable, but it is evident it will have an impact on both worlds on a planetary scale. The sub-probe has placed a mini-probe in uninhabited locations in the equatorial region of both worlds to assist with the monitoring of seismic activity during the crossing. The simulation indicates that both worlds will enter each other's gravity well in just over 4 Earth years from the date-stamp of the simulation. During this time period the sub-probe will continue to monitor the communication transmissions of the inhabitants of Gollredd for references to this event and their preparation activities for it. As initially reported, as all indications are that the species that inhabit Gollredd are unaware of life in the Universe outside of that of their own world, the sub-probe will monitor and document the planetary crossing of Teroknor, but will remain in its distant stationary satellite position and will make no attempt to make contact with the inhabitants of Gollredd.

Moonrise At Sunset At Emerald Rock Lake

Probe Evad's long-range scanners discovered a single planet in orbit around a brilliant Supergiant Star, 100 times larger than planet Earth's Sun and over one million times as bright. The single planet orbits its star at an average distance of just over 5.9 billion kilometers, just slightly more distant from its star than Pluto orbits the Sun of planet Earth's solar system. While similar in distance from its star as Pluto is from the Sun, this planet completes a single orbit of its star in just over 100 Earth years, which is less than half the time it takes Pluto to complete a single orbit. Probe Evad released a Level 3 sub-probe to investigate further.

Upon reaching full scanner capable range and establishing its observational satellite positioning, the sub-probe's initial long-range scans discovered that the planet has a single Moon. Its Moon is just slightly larger than 1/4 the diameter of the planet and the planet is a mere 100 kilometers larger in diameter than planet Earth. The distance between the planet and its Moon is 386,200 kilometers, which makes the Moon appear in the sky of the planet very similar as does the Moon of planet Earth, however, the sub-probe has discovered that unlike the Moon of planet Earth, this planet's Moon is not in orbit around the planet. Instead of the Moon orbiting the planet, the Moon and the planet are both seemingly in orbit around a central point between them. Also unlike the relationship of that between planet Earth and its Moon, both this planet and its Moon rotate. The planet, while just slightly larger in diameter than planet Earth, rotates on its axis more rapidly, completing a single rotation in the equivalent of 16 Earth hours. Its Moon rotates on its axis very rapidly, completing a single rotation in just over the equivalent of 2 Earth hours. The planet and its Moon complete a single orbital cycle around their common central point in approximately 32 Earth hours. This orbital cycle causes the Star to appear to pulsate in the planet's sky as the planet travels between its nearest and furthest distance from the Star during the orbital cycle with its Moon. This orbital cycle between the planet and its Moon creates the most rapid new Moon to full Moon cycle ever documented and the dynamics of the gravitational forces that maintains this unusual orbital relationship, as well as how their joint rapid orbit around this Supergiant Star is maintained, is as of yet unknown.

The sub-probe's long-range topographical scans have revealed the planet to be extremely Earth-like with an almost identical volume of liquid water to that found on planet Earth. The bio-life scans have discovered that the planet is inhabited by an abundant number of diverse life forms including a dominant bi-pedal humanoid species physiologically similar to that of humankind. Initial scans detected no activity whatsoever in orbit around the planet or its Moon. Secondary scans of the planet's surface detected an extensive network of roadways, housing structures ranging in size from very small, apparent single occupant dwellings, to massive complexes located in extremely densely populated city centers and the secondary bio-life scans have estimated the bi-pedal humanoid population to be in excess of 9 billion inhabitants. A sophisticated communications network is apparently in place, as a multitude of extremely high frequency transmissions, similar to the microwave transmissions used in the past on planet Earth have been intercepted, however, as of yet, the sub-probe has been unable to determine how the transmissions are being sent and received as no apparent transmission towers or power transfer stations have been identified.

The sub-probe's onboard linguistic compilers have completed their initial evaluation of this world's extremely complicated language structure based upon the communication transmissions that have been intercepted thus far. The initial English translation of their language has determined that the name the inhabitants have given to their world is Greewatoublak. It has also been determined that the inhabitants that have been identified as this world's scientists, are unaware of intelligent life outside of their own world. Construction and testing is underway for their first attempts at space travel and have chosen their Moon as their initial major destination objective. Very similar to humankind's initial space explorations, this world's scientists have scheduled a series of non-piloted orbital test flights in preparation for their piloted test flights and ultimate mission of landing a team on their Moon. Due to their upcoming tests and ongoing observations of their Moon, the sub-probe will remain at its current long-range observational satellite position and will make no attempt at first contact at this time.

The sub-probe's long-range topographical scans have documented extensive organized agricultural activities primarily located on the largest northern landmass of the planet. Atmospheric scans have documented the atmosphere of the planet to be very similar to planet Earth, with the major differences being a much higher concentration of hydrogen and oxygen. Even with the multitude of large industrial complexes located on the planet's surface the concentration of greenhouse gases in the planet's atmosphere are very minimal. The long-range surface technological scans have identified several enormous facilities located in various bodies of water, all within .1 kilometer of the shorelines of the most densely populated landmasses, as power generation facilities. Large amounts of steam is being expelled from tube-like structures extending skyward from the facilities. It is speculated that the release of steam from all of the identified power plants is largely responsible for the high concentrations of hydrogen and oxygen in the atmosphere. The power being generated by the facilities is transferred to apparent distribution facilities on shore via underwater/ underground pipelines and is literally identical in nature to the electricity as used on planet Earth.

The modes of transportation utilized by the inhabitants of the planet are limited to the surface of the planet and range from small vehicles, similar to the automobiles of twenty-first century planet Earth, to very large transport vehicles, similar to many of planet Earth's mass-transit systems, some of which, bio-life scans estimate to be carrying thousands of inhabitants. The difference between the land-based vehicles of this world and those found on planet Earth is that the land-based vehicles of this world have no wheels. Instead of making physical contact with the surface, this world's land-based vehicles levitate approximately 150 millimeters above the surface and maneuver making little to no sound. How the vehicles are being levitated or being propelled are as of yet unknown. There are a multitude of forms of transportation for traveling upon and in the liquid water of the planet's surface. On the surface, the methods of transportation range from individual and minimal capacity crafts to enormous transports similar in appearance to the historic riverboat steamships of nineteenth century Earth, including huge circular paddlewheels at the rear of the transports. The large transports have similar tube-like structures extending skyward like those of the identified power generation facilities and technological scans have confirmed that these crafts self-generate the power needed for their propulsion. Bio-life scans have documented that the largest transports have occupant capacities of nearly 14,000 passengers. Submarine-like crafts of varying sizes have been documented primarily in the vicinities of the power generation facilities and appear to only be in use for the construction and maintenance of the facilities or for scientific research, thus far none have been observed being utilized for general transportation or recreational purposes.

The long-range atmospheric scans have documented many large and turbulent rainstorms due to the high concentration of hydrogen and oxygen in the atmosphere. Due to the volume of steam being expelled into the atmosphere by the power generation facilities and large transportation vehicles that travel the planet's liquid water surface, powerful updrafts occur that generate extremely windy conditions in the upper atmosphere of the planet. As these updrafts collide with the prevailing winds of the planet many of the storms are accompanied by enormous swirling electrical discharges that light up the sky with intensely bright green lightning bolts, some of which swirl and streak across the sky for hundreds of kilometers.

The most recent long-range topographical scans have documented an unusual anomaly on the surface of the planet as well. The mountain range lake of the southern landmass on the planet Greewatoublak glows a fluorescent green each day during the planet's moonrise at sunset. The planet's scientists have been unable to determine the cause of this phenomenon, nor duplicate this effect under laboratory conditions. The closest English translation of the name given to the lake by the inhabitants of the planet is Emerald Rock Lake.

As previously reported, the sub-probe will remain at its current long-range observational satellite position, will continue to observe this world and study the extremely complicated language structure of its inhabitants, as well as document their space exploration activities. No attempt at first contact will be made until more is understood about the culture of this world's inhabitants and their reasons and intensions regarding space travel.

.07
The Steel Pyramid Of Golden Range

Probe Evad received an audio transmission being transmitted via an extremely high frequency, which was identified to be originating from a planet nearly a light-year away. Probe Evad released a Level 3 sub-probe to investigate. En route to the planet, the sub-probe continued to receive the methodically repeating transmission consisting of just eight sounds/words. One of the eight sounds/words of the transmission, speculated to be the name given to this world, is Sundooplun.

Upon entering initial scanner range of the planet, the sub-probe activated its long-range technological, topographical and bio-life scanners. The long-range technological scans were unable to determine the precise source of the audio transmission, nor were they able to detect any form of technology on the surface, or in orbit around the planet whatsoever. The long-range topographical scans documented no vegetation, nor was any liquid of any kind detected on the surface of the planet. The long-range bio-life scanners detected no life form readings of any kind on the surface, in the atmosphere, or in orbit around the planet. This planet is one of only two planets in orbit around a white dwarf star. The companion planet, which orbits this star much more closely than does Sundooplun, is a very small heavily cratered world. The sub-probe's long-range scans have established that this small world is composed of solid rock, with an inactive core, has no atmosphere and does not rotate as it orbits the star. The long-range bio-life scans have also detected no life forms of any kind on its surface or in orbit. While all of the long-range scans indicated that there were no life forms or technology on either world, the repetitious transmission continued to appear to be originating from Sundooplun. Upon completion of all long-range scans of the two planets, the sub-probe set a course for an equatorial orbit of the planet Sundooplun.

Upon establishing orbit of the planet, the sub-probe began extensive scans of the planet's surface. The short-range topographical scans indicate that the planet is a hot, desert world, with its entire surface consisting of very dense, fine granular sand. The short-range scans confirmed the findings of the long-range scans and no vegetation or liquid of any kind can be located on the planet's surface. The atmosphere of the planet is extremely thin and consists of small traces of sulfur and carbon dioxide, as well as sand particles lifted up from the planet's surface by the prevailing winds. The short-range bio-life scans were also unable to locate any life forms on the planet's surface, in the atmosphere, or in orbit of the planet. As the sub-probe was now in orbit, it was evident that the transmission was indeed being sent from somewhere on, or from beneath the surface of Sundooplun, as the strength of the signal was now very strong. The sub-probe released a mini-probe into a low progressively altering orbit to systematically scan and map the entire surface of the planet.

The only structure that can be detected on the sand-covered surface of the planet Sundooplun is a pyramid-shaped structure composed of a material similar in molecular composition to that of steel used on planet Earth, with the exception of the extreme density of its molecules. Due to this molecular density, none of the onboard scanners, sensors or mini-probes have been able to penetrate its surface. Also, due to the fine granular composition of the sand that makes up the planet's surface, the exact size of the pyramid cannot be determined. Its purpose, or contents if any, is as of yet, unknown.

The continued evaluation of the repeating eight sounds/words of the transmission being sent from this world has yielded little else than the speculation that Sundooplun is the name that has been given to this planet. It is as of yet unclear as to whether this transmission is a beacon or a warning, or whether it is of a friendly or hostile intent. Thus far, the key factor towards being unable to identify the origin of the transmission has been that the signal strength of the transmission has been identical regardless of the orbital position of the sub-probe or any of the released mini-probes. The most recently released mini-probe landed on the surface just 4.3 meters from the exposed base of the steel-like pyramid. Even at this close proximity to the pyramid, the fine granular composition of the sand has made it impossible for the onboard ground-penetrating radar to determine the exact size of the pyramid. However, since this most recent landing on the surface, the analysis of the sand based upon the samples taken by the landed mini-probe, have provided the orbiting sub-probe with a much more in-depth understanding of the molecular composition of the sand. As there is only one remaining mini-probe aboard the sub-probe that is capable of landing on the planet's surface, as well as was the only included mini-probe capable of burrowing down into a planet's surface in its entirety, the sub-probe has cleared this mini-probe's initial programming and has reprogrammed it with an entirely new set of instructional directives. This mini-probe, like its predecessor, will once again land within close proximity to the pyramid. The sub-probe has repositioned itself in a geostationary orbit directly above the pyramid to maintain direct line-of-sight positioning with this mini-probe, so as to establish and maintain the strongest possible communications signal with it.

Once landed, this mini-probe will separate itself from its landing module and maneuver itself to a perpendicular positioning to a side of the pyramid at its base. Once in position, the mini-probe will maneuver up the side of the pyramid until all of its wheels are in full contact with the surface of the pyramid. When this full contact is established, the mini-probe will activate the wheel's as well as, its base's magnetic enhancement, ensuring the mini-probe remains in contact and properly oriented to the pyramid, as it bores its way into the surface of the planet while traversing the side of the pyramid. While as of yet, none of the scanners or sensors onboard the sub-probe or mini-probes have been able to penetrate the surface of the pyramid in order to determine its contents, nor have they been able to determine its size due to the fine granular composition of the sand that makes up the planet's surface, it is anticipated the communication signal should now be capable of penetrating the surface of the planet for several miles. The sub-probe has reprogrammed the mini-probe's directives and communications protocols, completed the magnetic enhancements to the mini-probe's wheels and base and is performing all of the final pre-release diagnostics of the mini-probe's mission objective instructional sets. Based upon what was learned as a result of the most recent molecular composition tests of the sand on the surface of Sundooplun, it is anticipated that the mini-probe should have no difficulty burrowing its way into the surface while maintaining physical contact with the pyramid, nor should its updated communication protocols have any difficulty remaining in contact with the orbiting sub-probe as it descends into the planet's surface. As none of the other mini-probe's in orbit around the planet have detected any other structures or technology anywhere else on the surface of the planet, the sub-probe has redirected all but one mini-probe to concentrate its investigations on the pyramid and its surrounding area. The one remaining mini-probe will stay in its current progressively altering orbit and will continue to systematically scan the entire surface of the planet, continuing to monitor for any type of activity whatsoever anywhere else on the planet's surface during the intensified examinations of the pyramid. When the sub-probe completed the mission directive updates of all of the currently deployed mini-probes, it then completed its review of the final pre-release diagnostics of the remaining exploratory mini-probe and began the release sequence for its landing on the surface.

The release of the mini-probe was flawless as was the activation of all of its onboard computer systems. Once the sub-probe received the mini-probe's onboard navigation system's trajectory data receipt acknowledgement, the sub-probe initiated the mini-probe's descent sequence. The mini-probe engaged its de-orbital thrusters and began its descent to the planet's surface. The mini-probe's initial entry into the planet's upper atmosphere was near perfect, however, during its descent the mini-probe encountered unexpected turbulence, which quickly began to send it off course. After a series of dramatic course corrections, remarkably, the mini-probe landed a mere 8 meters from the base of the pyramid.

Once on the surface, the mini-probe successfully separated itself from its landing module and performed all of its internal diagnostic tests and established an extremely strong communications link with the orbiting sub-probe.

Fortunately, while the mini-probe experienced a difficult descent, all of its systems appear to be in excellent working condition. Upon completing all of its arrival tests and reporting, the mini-probe maneuvered itself to the base of the pyramid. It activated its onboard magnetic systems and began its ascent up the side of the pyramid. Once all of its wheels were in contact with the pyramid it stopped its ascent, activated its burrowing mechanisms and began its descent into the planet's surface. The orbiting sub-probe will continue to monitor the progress of this mini-probe, as well as all of the other deployed mini-probes, in the attempt to determine the purpose of the pyramid and reason for its placement on this desolate world.

Preparing To Dock At Odean 3

Probe Evad detected an enormous planetary system consisting of a total of 31 planets in orbit around a single Dwarf Star, which is just slightly larger than 3 times the size of the Sun of planet Earth's solar system. As probe Evad's long-range scans detected a great deal of bio-life activity within the system and with this planetary system consisting of so many planets, probe Evad elected to fabricate a secondary mini-probe storage and launch module and a Level 3 sub-probe that would investigate the system in tandem. Probe Evad's fabrication module first fabricated the secondary module and equipped it with a wide array of mini-probes, more than tripling the number of mini-probes that would be available to this sub-probe for investigating this system. Upon its completion, the secondary module was released and placed in a standby flight position within the gravitational tow range of probe Evad while the fabrication of the Level 3 sub-probe took place. Due to the additional programming required to control the secondary module and the wide array of its additional onboard mini-probes, this sub-probe was the most sophisticated sub-probe probe Evad had fabricated thus far. When completed, the sub-probe was released and the complicated docking sequence that had never been attempted before was initiated. As the docking of the Level 3 sub-probe and the secondary module had to take place within the gravitational tow range of probe Evad, and with the extreme volatility of the two crafts due to the multitude of power sources of the large volume of mini-probes onboard, this was an extremely dangerous, tremendously time consuming process, as an accident had the potential of causing irreparable damage to probe Evad. Fortunately, due to the extremely sophisticated programming and extraordinary attention dedicated to safety, the docking maneuver transpired precisely as planned. However, while performing the systems diagnostics several of the mini-probes aboard the secondary module were non-responsive. Along with performing its scheduled long-range scans, the sub-probe will also continue to run diagnostics while en route to its target planetary system towards determining the cause and possible rectification of these mini-probe malfunctions.

As the sub-probe approached the planetary system, its long-range scans confirmed probe Evad's initial scans and documented a great deal of bio-life activity within the system. As per its mission directives, when the sub-probe reached full scanner capable range of the outermost planet of the system where bio-life could be detected, it activated its first contact observational protocols and engaged its propulsion system to de-accelerate to its all-stop initial observational satellite position. When the sub-probe achieved its all-stop position, it activated the remainder of its onboard scanners. From this observational satellite position the sub-probe was capable of scanning the entire planetary system with its enhanced short-range scanners. Upon completing its initial full system bio-life scan, the sub probe detected bio-life on 28 of the 31 planets of this system, as well as on a multitude of the Moons in orbit around them. Due to the extreme density of bio-life signs on some of the planets, as well as the high volume of instances of detected underground activity, not only on many of the planets but on the multitude of Moons as well, the total number of inhabitants of this planetary system is currently incalculable. The only detected species of this system is a bi-pedal humanoid species similar in stature to humankind, however, thus far, no visible distinction as to any variance in race has been identified. With the exception of very subtle differences in appearance and height, all of the inhabitants of this system look virtually identical. They all have two hazy-white colored eyes which are approximately twice the height and four times the width of those of humankind and are spaced much more widely apart, wrapping slightly to the sides of their heads with no detectable pupils. They have extremely small mouths and no detectable ears or nose. Their skin is blue-grey in color with no detectable hair or genitalia, and no observance of the use of any form of clothing, jewelry or body markings has been made. The initial short-range bio-life scans were unable to determine any gender difference or any indication of how their species is propagated. Surprisingly, other than this bi-pedal species, initial short-range scans have been unable to detect or document any other life forms whatsoever anywhere within this planetary system.

It was initially speculated that the sub-probe's communication system and onboard linguistic compilers were malfunctioning, as while a great deal of apparent communication signals were detected, no audio of any kind in any known frequency range could be identified. The short-range technological scans finally established that the detected communication signals are extremely high-speed, multi-layered, highly compressed video-based communications. After evaluating several thousand transmissions, the linguistic compilers have determined that the inhabitants of this planetary system have no spoken or sound-based language, no audible method of communication, nor have any references been found indicating that the inhabitants possess any form of telepathic abilities. Their physical form of communication consists of extremely rapid hand gestures, similar to the sign language used by the deaf on planet Earth. Their written language is a multi-colored, symbol-based language, of which, transmissions have been intercepted being sent and responded to at extraordinarily high speeds. It is apparent that the inhabitants of this planetary system possess very sophisticated visual and mental acuity. Once the linguistic compilers had established the two main forms of communication, extensive evaluation of both forms of the intercepted transmissions began towards translating the language structures and developing not only first contact messages, but also formulating a methodology for communicating with the inhabitants of this system in this unusual manner and at the extraordinarily high speeds in which their transmissions are exchanged.

When the sub-probe's onboard linguistic compilers completed their initial evaluations and translations of the language structures utilized by the inhabitants of this system, it was determined that the inhabitants had named their planetary system Odean. Unlike that of other planetary systems, including humankind's, as opposed to giving unique names to each of the planets, the inhabitants have assigned numerical designations to each of the planets based upon the order in which they were colonized. A reference was found that the inhabitant's home world, the twelfth planet from this system's Star, was initially named Odean. Upon the colonization of the first planet beyond their home world, the fifteenth planet from this system's Star, which they named Odean 2, the inhabitants of this system renamed their home world Odean 1 and began referring to their entire planetary system as Odean. Based on references from data gathered thus far, the inhabitants of the Odean system first left their home world and began their exploration and colonization of the planets of their Star System just over 400 Earth years ago. As initially reported, thus far the Odean's have colonized 28 of the 31 planets of their system as well as many of the Moons in orbit around them. The first and closest planet to this system's Star is a very small, extremely hot barren world that orbits this system's Star at an astonishing rate. While the Odean's have landed a small craft on its surface for scientific research purposes, due to the extreme surface temperatures and brightness caused by its close proximity to the Star, indications are that the Odean's have no intention of ever colonizing this world. The second planet from this system's Star is a huge gas giant, which is just 100 kilometers larger in diameter than the planet Jupiter of planet Earth's solar system and is nearly twice the distance from this system's Star as planet Earth is from its Sun. The speculation is that had this world been a bit larger it might have exploded into a stellar companion to this system's Star. Due to the extreme atmospheric pressures and no detectable solid surface the Odean's have classified this world as uninhabitable. The 31st and furthest planet from this system's Star is a world roughly 3 times the size of planet Earth. Its surface is made up of primarily frozen methane with a thin atmosphere also mostly composed of methane. Its average surface temperature is -230° C. While the Odean's have several research crafts on the planet's surface, all indications thus far are that the research being performed is towards the viability of mining the frozen methane as a possible fuel source and not, due to the extremely cold surface temperature, towards the feasibility of the planet for colonization purposes.

Construction has been completed on the outpost built on Odean 3. It is thus far the largest known facility of its kind, capable of supporting 260,000 inhabitants. Its construction also required the largest known investment in labor ever invested in facility construction. In total worker hours, took 72 years, 9 months, 14 days, 6 hours, 23 minutes and 54.1 seconds. This outpost is now the main technological and supply depot for the entire Odean System. While the name given to this world is Odean 3, it is the 16th planet from the system's Star and its orbit around the Star is located at nearly the precise center of the Odean system.

The sub-probe has completed the preparation of its initial first contact messages and is now making its final preparations for entry into the system and initiating contact with the Odean's.

.09
Saucer Patrol Of Tendril

   While performing general long-range scans of a group of three cool-red Dwarf Stars located in close proximity to one another, probe Evad intercepted a short audio transmission. The precise origin of the intercepted transmission could not be determined and was of insufficient length to determine any form of language structure or to be able to compile any type of definitive translation. However, as the transmission was intercepted while performing the general long-range scans of the three cool-red Dwarf Stars, probe Evad began extensive long-range scans of them. Upon doing so, a single planet was detected in a distant, unusually patterned orbit around the three Stars. Probe Evad fabricated and released a Level 3 sub-probe to investigate.
   As the sub-probe entered its initial long-range scanner distance from the planet, the sub-probe discovered that the

planet was in fact not a planet, but was instead, a large Moon, roughly 4 times the size of planet Earth, in orbit around an extremely large dark planet roughly 10 times the size of the Moon. While en route to the planet, the sub-probe's onboard linguistic compiler's ongoing review of the intercepted audio transmission has led the sub-probe to speculate that the one repeated word, Tendril, is the name that has been given to this world and until determined otherwise, the sub-probe will refer to it as such for the purposes of reporting its findings during its investigation of it. Other than the discovery of the planet Tendril itself, the long-range scans have been unable to acquire any readings of the planet other than the long-range technological scan's detection of a fluctuating electromagnet field that encompasses the planet. The sub-probe ran complete system-wide diagnostics on all long-range scanners and upon completion, performed a second series of all long-range scans of the planet as well as its Moon. Once again, other than the fluctuating electromagnet field that encompasses the entire planet, no other form of technology or bio-life activity could be detected on the surface of the planet or the Moon, nor in orbit of either one. The sub-probe plotted a course and engaged its engines embarking on the journey to its orbital destination of the planet.

As the sub-probe approached the planet, due to the planet's unexpected incredibly strong gravity well, the sub-probe had to make a series of quick flight trajectory adjustments in order to insert itself into a stable orbit. Also due to the planet's strong gravity well, in order to establish the consistent stable orbit, the sub-probe needed to adjust its orbit to nearly 300 kilometers further from the planet than initially selected. When the sub-probe finally established a stable orbit around the planet, it began its short-range scans. What upon approach to the planet visually appeared to be a dark, featureless barren surface, the short-range topographical and technological scans determined, as detected by its long-range scans, to be an electromagnetic field encompassing the entire planet. The technological scans have thus far been unable to determine the power source or method in which this planetary field is being generated. The sub-probe has launched a series of mini-probes into a lower orbit for closer inspection of the field and to acquire more precise readings of the planet's atmosphere. Thus far the topographical scanners have been unable to penetrate the electromagnet field, so the makeup and physical characteristics of the planet's surface is as of yet unknown. The short-range scans of the planet's Moon have found it to be very similar in composition and appearance to that of the Moon of planet Earth. Its surface is primarily made up of basalts and igneous rocks, as well as high concentrations of helium-3. No liquid of any kind was detected on the surface nor was any type of atmosphere found. Its surface is by comparison much more cratered than that of Earth's Moon. It is hypothesized that this is due to the enormous size of the planet and its extremely strong gravity well, which would have drawn in a great deal of stellar debris during the accretion phase of its creation, which would have resulted in much of the debris making impact with the Moon as well. Oddly, with respect to the Moon's overall size, if it too had been formed by an accretion process, it is projected that the Moon's core should contain much more iron than has been detected. Based on the short-range scans, and the ground penetrating radar scans that were performed by a mini-probe that was dispatched to more fully investigate the Moon, very little iron was detected at its core, unusual for a planetary satellite of its size. Also, due to it's small iron core and the fact that the Moon does not rotate upon its own axis, as it is locked in a stationery orbital position around the planet, which results in the same side of the Moon always facing the planet, also identically to that of planet Earth's Moon, this Moon has little to no gravity of its own. Bio-life scans have found that there is no bio-activity of any kind whatsoever on the surface of the Moon, nor thus far has any evidence been found that indicates that the Moon has ever supported any form of bio-life. The mini-probe that was dispatched for closer investigation of the Moon has found no evidence that any form of technology has ever explored its surface nor was any kind of technological device detected in orbit around it.

The mini-probes that the sub-probe had dispatched to investigate the planet from a lower planetary orbit have completed all of their initially programmed scans. The atmosphere contains high concentrations of nitrogen and two distinct cloud layers. The lower cloud layer consists of nitrogen gas and small concentrations of water vapor that forms a hazy thin broken cloud layer, which oddly, uniformly encompasses the entire planet at a height of approximately 10 kilometers from a dark non-translucent force-field-like shield of some kind. The upper cloud layer consists of sporadic large thick clouds made up of primarily nitrogen gas with small concentrations of frozen water vapor, which glow a brilliant red color caused by the cool-red rays of this system's three central Dwarf Stars. The upper cloud layer maintains a distance of approximately 30 kilometers from the lower cloud layer. The atmosphere between the two cloud layers contains the highest concentration of nitrogen along with, an as of yet unidentified gaseous compound. This central atmospheric layer also exhibits electromagnetic properties similar to the dark non-translucent force-field-like shield with the exception of its polarity being a near complete opposite. It is speculated that it is because of this opposite polarity, in conjunction with the as of yet unidentified gaseous compound, that at the planet's horizon it can be seen that this central atmospheric layer glows a brilliant fluorescent white, which can only be observed while in orbit around the planet within this central atmospheric layer. Multiple sightings of disk-shaped spacecraft, each sighting consisting of a formation of four crafts, were observed apparently patrolling the planet

Tendril in low orbit. Thus far the patrols have only been observed within the central atmospheric layer. No crafts have been observed outside of this central region, neither leaving orbit of the planet nor entering or exiting the dark non-translucent force-field-like shield. Due to the non-reply to attempts of communication, as well as the force fields that surround the spacecrafts, the identities of the spacecraft occupants or the purpose of the patrols is unknown. None of the on-board scanners, sensors or mini-probes were able to penetrate the force-field-like shield that also surrounds the planet. The planet's surface characteristics, species type and number of inhabitants are also unknown. It is speculated that the spacecrafts may be responsible for generating the planet's shield.

As the dispatched mini-probes had completed their initially programmed scans and the sub-probe had compiled all of the report data received from them, the sub-probe formulated a secondary set of instructional parameters for the mini-probes, primarily targeted towards making contact with the inhabitants of the spacecrafts as well as the presupposed planetary inhabitants. Within seconds of the sub-probe transmitting the secondary instructional sets to the mini-probes, simultaneously all communication links were lost to all of the mini-probes in orbit around the planet. As the sub-probe was unable to re-establish a communication link with any of the mini-probes, the sub-probe began short-range scans in an effort to locate and run system diagnostics on the mini-probes. No trace of any of the mini-probes could be found. The communication link with the mini-probe in orbit around the Moon is still intact and communications are working perfectly. The mini-probe in orbit around the Moon will be of no use towards investigating the planet however, as it has insufficient power to break free of the Moon's gravity and the planet is too far away for its onboard scanners to be of use. With the additional data gathered from the initial scans by the dispatched mini-probes along with the compiled data from the short-range scans by the sub-probe itself, the sub-probe established the necessary parameters and programmed the flight trajectory and navigational systems for entry into and the establishment of, a stable orbit around the planet within the central atmospheric region of the planet. Upon establishing its stable orbit within the central region, the sub-probe initiated its first contact broadcast. As with the mini-probes, within seconds of initiating its transmissions, the sub-probe's Communication Relay Pod lost all contact with the sub-probe. The status, or present location of the sub-probe, is currently unknown.

10

Orredpurblu Galaxy

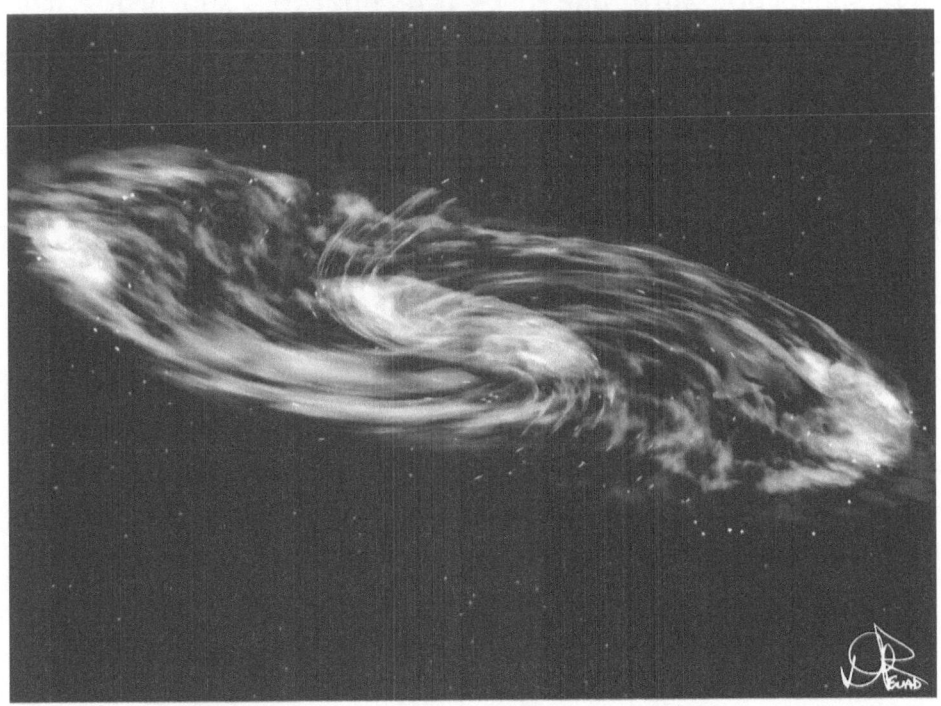

It is calculated that this view of the Orredpurblu Galaxy, due to its distance from probe Evad, is a view back in time of 14.26 billion years. At the edges of this galaxy, on opposite sides of its center, are extremely torrent sectors with high concentrations of the same molecular composites as those found at the Galaxy's center. Study of this Galaxy will continue in order to try to determine if these two torrents were somehow expelled from the Galaxy's center, or perhaps created as a result of some type of galactic collision and subsequent merging event. Due to the near incalculable distance this galaxy is from probe Evad, it would take hundreds of thousands of years for even the most sophisticated sub-probe that probe Evad could fabricate to reach it.

As probe Evad had such great success with the fabrication and merging of a secondary sub-probe, as it did with the sub-probes dispatched to explore the Odean System, probe Evad formulated the plan and procedures for merging a total of five sub-probes into one large interoperable sub-probe, for the tandem mission of observing and reporting its findings of the Orredpurblu Galaxy for as long of a period of time as possible. As the merging of two sub-probes was originally contemplated by DSEC scientists, but was determined to be too dangerous, the merging of a total of five sub-probe's is exponentially more dangerous and had the potential of not only severely damaging probe Evad, but risked causing its complete destruction. Probe Evad ran ten's of thousand's of simulations in the attempt to prepare for every possible malfunction that could take place during the assembly and release of this five-sub-probe tandem array. Upon completion of its final simulation, probe Evad determined that while indeed extremely dangerous, it could in fact safely accomplish the task and began its final preparations for the replication and assembly of this extraordinarily complicated sub-probe array. The array will consist of a total of five Level 3 sub-probes.

The first component probe Evad fabricated was the central sub-probe. As the primary mission of this sub-probe array is to study the Orredpurblu Galaxy, none of the sub-probes themselves will be equipped with short-range scanners. The only short-range scanners that will be available to the array will be those of the included mini-probes, for use in the event that an extraordinary point of interest arises while en route to the Orredpurblu Galaxy. With the addition of the four supplemental Level 3 sub-probes, the ability to track and monitor this sub-probe array has been significantly enhanced, as the four external sub-probe modules have been equipped with specially modified, linked Communication Relay Pods, that in conjunction, will relay the sub-probe array's exploratory data back to the main central sub-probe's Communication Relay Pod, which will remain in probe Evad's flight trajectory that was inserted into position when the sub-probe array was released. The central sub-probe will act as the sub-probe array's command module and contains no mini-probes of its own. In their place, probe Evad's fabrication module has greatly expanded and enhanced the central sub-probe's long-range scanners, data compilers, data storage systems and its long-range communications systems. Probe Evad also significantly expanded the array's main operational systems, which was required for its unprecedented ability to control the long-range scanners of the four external sub-probes, as well as coordinate and track the deployment of their onboard mini-probes.

When the fabrication of the central control sub-probe was complete, probe Evad released and placed it in a standby flight position within its gravitational tow range while the fabrication of the four external Level 3 sub-probes took place. As per probe Evad's formulated plan for the sub-probe array, due to the fact that none of the external sub-probes would be equipped with their own short-range scanners, each of the external sub-probes would be equipped with an extremely sophisticated and diverse series of mini-probes. In place of their individual short-range scanners, each external sub-probe was fabricated with enhanced data compilers, data storage systems and unprecedented multi-purpose communications systems. Each sub-probe's onboard communication system was not only enhanced to be able to independently deploy, track and monitor its own mini-probes, but was also enhanced with the capability of working in tandem with the main central sub-probe's communication system towards extending the sub-probe array's overall communication range. Each external sub-probe was fabricated with its own Communication Relay Pod, which were also enhanced with special linking protocols, giving them the ability to transfer communication data transmissions from the main central sub-probe's communication system, linked sequentially to one another with final communication link to the main central sub-probe's Communication Relay Pod, which will remain within probe Evad's flight trajectory.

Due to the extreme danger associated with assembling such a large sub-probe array within the gravitational tow range of probe Evad, as the fabrication of each sub-probe was completed, probe Evad dedicated all of its control and communication systems, with the exception of its own internal flight trajectory systems, towards controlling and monitoring the positioning and docking of each external sub-probe to the main central sub-probe. Once an external sub-probe had acknowledged that a secure docking had been accomplished, probe Evad then began the fabrication of the next external sub-probe, repeating the process until the fourth and final external sub-probe was securely docked with the main central sub-probe, completing the assembly of the sub-probe array. While all of the systems and mini-probes of each external sub-probe was extensively tested prior to being released, once the assembly of the entire sub-probe array was complete, probe Evad ran several hundred thousand system and communication tests to ensure all of the systems of the sub-probe array were functioning as programmed and properly communicating with the main central sub-probe. When these tests were completed, probe Evad ran a multitude of system and communication tests on the main central sub-probe, to ensure that it not only had definitive communication and control of all of the external sub-probe systems as well as proper communication links to all of the external sub-probe's Communication Relay Pods, but that they also had a positive link to its own Communication Relay Pod and then confirmed communication link with probe Evad, as well as all of the other previously deployed Communication Relay Pods. Upon the successful completion of all of the diagnostic tests, probe Evad began the sub-probe array's pre-release sequence.

Due to the enormous size of the sub-probe array, the most dangerous procedure of this unprecedented undertaking was the release of the sub-probe array from probe Evad's gravitational tow range. As releasing a sub-probe of the enormous size and mass of that of the sub-probe array had never been contemplated, the effect, if any, that the sub-probe array's release from probe Evad's gravitational tow range would have upon probe Evad's flight trajectory was unknown. Probe Evad had run thousand's of simulations towards finalizing the sub-probe array's release sequence. It was determined from the simulations that a precisely timed series of procedures would need to be executed in order to ensure the safety of both the sub-probe array and probe Evad, as well as to maintain the integrity of probe Evad's flight trajectory, while engaging the sub-probe array's engines at the precise moment in order to ensure the sub-probe array would be inserted into the proper trajectory towards the Orredpurblu Galaxy.

First, due to the enormous size and mass of the sub-probe array, probe Evad reduced its gravitational tow field to two thirds full intensity instead of the normal sub-probe release setting of one half intensity to begin the release sequence. As the sub-probe array began to slowly fall back from its assembly and tow position along side of probe Evad, the main central sub-probe released its Communication Relay Pod, which will remain within the flight trajectory of probe Evad. Second, when the sub-probe array had fallen back just beyond probe Evad's ion-plasma propulsion system, the sub-probe array initiated its engine start up sequences placing all five of its engines in full standby mode, making them ready for instant engine engagement. Finally, when the sub-probe array's engines had reached full standby mode and the sub-probe array had fallen back completely clear of probe Evad's ion-plasma propulsion system, simultaneously probe Evad disengaged the gravitational tow field as the sub-probe array engaged its engines. The instant the sub-probe array had cleared the range of probe Evad's gravitational tow field probe Evad immediately reactivated the field. The simultaneous actions instantly placed the sub-probe array into its trajectory towards the Orredpurblu Galaxy and the sub-probe array release had no effect on the flight trajectory of probe Evad. The release of the sub-probe array was a flawless operational success. The sub-probe array, now on its way towards the Orredpurblu Galaxy, has sufficient power and with the enhanced linked Communication Relay Pods, will be capable of delivering its reports for just over 2,500 years, far short of the time it would take to get there, but will provide an extraordinary amount of research and scientific data about this Galaxy.

11

Rotational Moon Demise

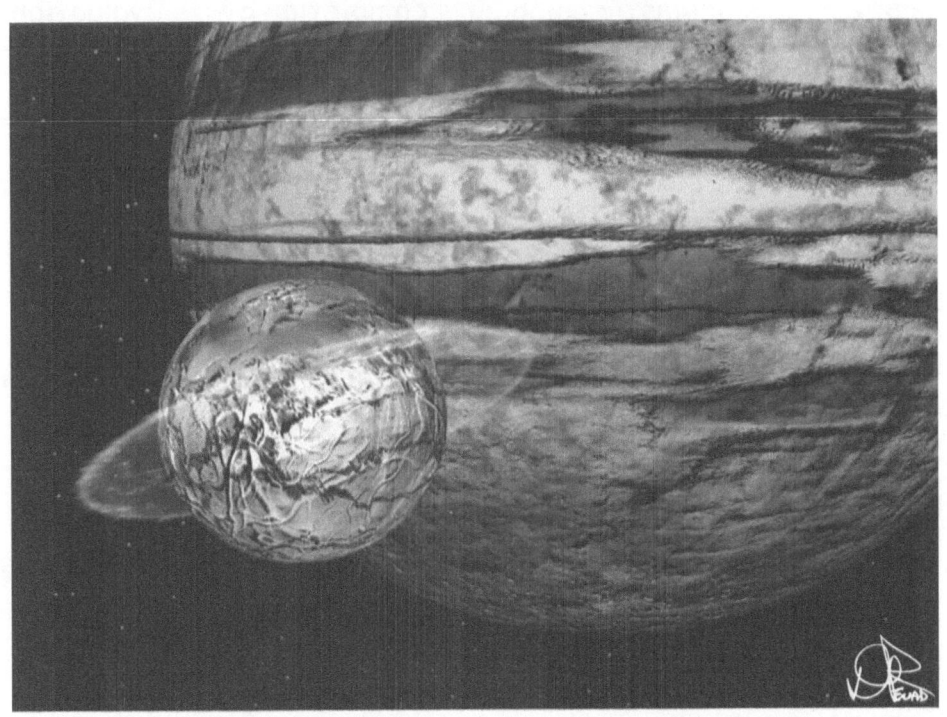

Probe Evad's long-range communication system intercepted a transmission, the exact origin of which could not be determined, however, the length of the transmission was sufficient for the onboard linguistic compilers to hypothesize a translation. The intent of the transmission was determined to be a warning regarding a planetary system with extremely powerful and dangerous gravitational forces. Upon triangulating the trajectory of the intercepted transmission, probe Evad's long-range scanners detected a planetary system consisting of six enormous planets in orbit around a Brown Dwarf Star calculated to be 71 times the mass of that of the planet Jupiter of Earth's planetary system. While probe Evad's long-range bio-life scanners detected no bio-life within the planetary system, due to the intercepted transmission, the likelihood of some form of communicative bio-life, either within or nearby this system, justified dispatching minimally a Level 2 sub-probe. Upon probe Evad's linguistic compiler's completion of its evaluation of the intercepted transmission, it was determined that the name given to this system is Dargrecol. Probe Evad performed enhanced secondary long-range scans of the system, however, once again, no bio-life of any kind was detected within the planetary system. The secondary scans did however confirm extremely strong gravitational fields within this system, subsequently, probe Evad enhanced the Level 2 sub-probe with additional maneuvering thrusters as well as equipped the majority of its on-board mini-probes with enhanced navigational and propulsion systems for optimal reliability within this gravitationally unstable planetary system.

When the sub-probe reached full scanner capable range of the planetary system, it activated its first contact observational protocols and engaged its propulsion system to de-accelerate to its all-stop initial observational satellite position. Upon completing all of its long-range scans of the system, as was the case with probe Evad's long-range scans, no bio-life of any kind was detected on any of the planets or the multitude of Moons in orbit around them. The sub-probe's scans also determined that the gravitational forces being generated by the six enormous planets of this system were too extreme and unstable to navigate and maneuver within the system itself. Instead, the sub-probe plotted a course putting it in position centered above the planetary orbital plane in line with the system's central Brown Dwarf Star. Due to the extremely low energy and light output of this system's star, this planetary system is the coldest and darkest planetary system discovered thus far. Another unusual feature of this system is that all six planets are almost identical in size and mass, the largest variance between them being a mere three kilometers in diameter with a minimal difference in overall mass. Much of this system's unstable gravitational forces are being generated by the extreme speeds in which these enormous planets orbit their central star. The most unusual and unexplainable planetary orbit is that of the third planet from the central star, which even though it orbits the star at a distance of nearly four times of that of the closest planet to the star, it orbits the star in just under half the amount of time, completing a single orbit in the equivalent to 572 Earth days. For comparison purposes, this planet orbits its star at a distance of nearly eight times of that of planet Earth's distance from the Sun. It is also the only planet of this system that has no orbiting Moons.

While planets discovered within other systems that are as enormous as the six planets of this planetary system are typically gas giants, such is not the case with the Dargrecol system. The first and closest planet to this system's central star has a solid iron core and an exceptionally smooth silicate based surface. Extremely rare for the closest planet to its star, is its total absence of any craters. In fact, the mini-probe dispatched to more closely examine this planet discovered that the surface of this planet is almost completely level, with the largest variance in altitude being less than one meter. The mini-probe also discovered that the planet has no discernible atmosphere of any kind. It is speculated the smooth silicate surface is maintained due to the combination of the planet's lack of atmosphere and powerful gravity generated by its solid iron core. The planet also rotates exceptionally slowly for a planet of its size completing a single rotation in the equivalent to 200 Earth days. The planet has one orbiting Moon, which is approximately twice the size of Earth's Moon that maintains a perfect circular orbit due to the fact that it is locked in a geostationary orbit around the planet. Due to the Moon's orbital positioning and the powerful gravitational forces of the planet, the Moon itself does not rotate. The mini-probe's long-range scans of this Moon have found the Moon to be as featureless as the planet itself, which is composed of the identical silicate, except that the Moon's silicate is frozen solid and the Moon has no detectable core of any kind.

The second planet from the central star has the most orbiting Moons of the six planets of this system with a total of 41. It is also the only planet of this system that does not rotate on a consistent axis. Instead, this planet rapidly irregularly tumbles through space as it traverses its orbital plane around the central star. The gravitational forces exerted upon it by the 41 orbiting Moons, none of which orbit the planet within the same orbital plane, perpetuate the tumbling of the planet. The surface of the planet is primarily composed of sulfurous molten rock and liquid metals and is dotted with thousands of pancake volcanoes, which are speculated to be collapsed domes over large magma chambers caused by the planet's extremely powerful gravity and rapid tumbling rotation. The atmosphere is a toxic mixture of sulfur dioxide, hydrogen sulfide, hydrogen chloride and carbon monoxide, which rapidly encompass the planet with wind speeds that average 1,300 kilometers per hour. The combination of the continual erupting volcanoes and the sulfurous molten rock and liquid metals which are expelled, this planet is the only hot planet of the system with a mean surface temperature of 715 K. It has been hypothesized that due to the gravitational forces exerted upon the planet by the 41 orbiting Moons, the potential exists that these forces will eventually tear the planet apart, causing not only the total destruction of the planet, but would then result in catastrophic consequences for the entire planetary system.

The fourth planet from this system's central star has been the most difficult of the six to further explore. The first two mini-probes that were dispatched to orbit this planet for closer examination crashed on the planet's surface due to this planet's extremely strong magnetic field. Upon planet approach, the second dispatched mini-probe was able to send critical field data back to the sub-probe, which allowed the sub-probe to calculate alternative orbital insertion parameters for the third mini-probe that was dispatched. While these programming adjustments prevented the orbital insertion failure as experienced by the first two mini-probes, the third mini-probe was only able to complete just over four orbits of the planet before it too crashed on the surface due to the exceptionally strong and erratic gravitational forces of the planet. However, prior to its crash, the third mini-probe had discovered that this planet's erratic magnetic fields are primarily a result of the planet's rotation being at a precise 90° angle to the central star with its poles perpendicular to the central star and parallel with its orbital plane. Also contributing to the planet's powerful magnetic field is its enormous iron core. The limited short-range scans that the third mini-probe was able to complete prior to its crash found the planet to be composed of iron sulfides, pyrite and extremely nickel-rich bravoite, giving the planet's surface a combination of glistening gold and red colors. The planet has two Moons that orbit it at nearly exact opposite sides of the planet at its equator and inexplicably, orbit the planet in the opposite direction of its rotation.

The second last planet in the Dargrecol system, is an extremely cold, dark world, with a thin toxic acid atmosphere and bodies of liquid acid oceans hundreds of times the size of planet Earth. The planet is so enormous that its gravity well is going to destroy its innermost three Moons. The rotation of the closest Moon continues to increase, as its orbit around the planet continues to decay. Based on data regarding the Moon debris and acids being expelled into space from its equator, it is speculated that the Moon will break apart from the extreme gravitational forces caused by its rapid rotation, prior to impacting the planet.

The last and by far the coldest planet of this system, is a world composed of frozen nitrogen, methane, ethane and carbon monoxide. It has an almost non-existent atmosphere containing only minute traces of nitrogen and carbon monoxide. This planet is the slowest rotating planet of the system completing a single rotation in the equivalent to just over 420 Earth days. There are 8 large irregular shaped Moons in a slow distant orbit around the planet, all of which are identical in composition. It is speculated that the 8 Moons are the result of a cataclysmic impact with this planet's Moon in its distant past. Due to the planet's slow rate of rotation and subsequently the slow orbit of and distance between the Moon fragments, there appears to be insufficient gravity for the Moon fragments to coalesce.

12

The Bronze Huts Of Teti

Probe Evad's long-range scans detected a high volume of communication transmissions originating from a planetary system consisting of a single White Dwarf central star with three orbiting planets. Due to the high volume of communication transmissions probe Evad dispatched a Level 3 sub-probe to investigate. When the sub-probe reached full scanner capable range, it activated its first contact observational protocols and engaged its propulsion system to de-accelerate to its all-stop initial observational satellite position, positioning itself just outside the orbital gravitational field of the furthermost planet from the central star. When the sub-probe achieved its all-stop positioning it performed its initial long and short-range scans of the entire planetary system.

The initial scans found the system to contain three planets orbiting the central star in nearly perfect alignment. The first and closest planet to the central star is an extremely volcanically active world roughly 30 times the size of planet Earth. The second planet is a rocky, mountainous planet roughly 10 times the size of planet Earth with a lower atmosphere, which is nearly identical to that of Earth. The third and final planet of this system is an enormous gas giant which is nearly 17 times the size of the planet Jupiter of Earth's solar system. Due to their sustained nearly perfect orbital alignment, an unusual multiple planetary phenomenon is taking place. As the thousands of volcanoes erupt on the first planet, planetary debris is ejected high into the planet's upper atmosphere, which due to the extremely strong gravitational forces of the third planet, is pulled from the first planet's upper atmosphere, showering the second planet in repeated meteor showers as the third planet devours the remainder of the first planet's volcanic ejections like an enormous vacuum cleaner. Due to the volume of meteors that enter the atmosphere of the second planet, the second planet's upper atmosphere cycles through periods of being thick with sulfuric smoke and debris as a result of the partial disintegrations of the meteoric bombardments, to then being purified by the high winds caused as the gravity of the third planet also draws the remaining debris from the second planet's upper atmosphere. It is as of yet unknown how the third planet is able to remove the smoke and debris from the second planet's upper atmosphere without removing the upper atmosphere in its entirety, nor how the second planet's lower atmosphere is remaining intact during these violent upper atmospheric cleansing cycles. It is also as of yet unknown how the first two planets of this system are able to maintain their orbital integrities around the central star with the strong gravitational forces that are being generated by the third planet.

The sub-probe's long-range scans of this system have determined that the intercepted communication transmissions are originating from the second planet. The sub-probe's long-range bio-life scans have also detected intermittent bio-life activity on the planet's surface, however no bio-life activity has been detected in orbit around the planet, nor has any spacecraft activity whatsoever been detected within the planetary system. All three planets rotate in a counter-clockwise direction at near perfect perpendicular positioning relative to their orbital planes around the central star. As the sub-probe's initial observational satellite positioning just outside the orbital gravitational field of the furthermost planet was beyond its short-range scanner range of the second planet, in order to fully investigate this world the sub-probe needed to either orbit the second planet or position itself within its short-range scanner range.

Due to the planetary debris being drawn from the first two planets by the third planet, the debris field created by this planetary phenomenon made a standard equatorial or geostationary orbit of the second planet by the sub-probe impossible. Due to the combination of the second planet's unusual magnetic field, as well as the strong gravitational forces of the third planet, sustaining a stable standard polar orbit was also not possible. Positioning itself directly in front of the second planet in line with its orbital path around the central star and yet remain within its short-range scanner range was also not a practical option, as maintaining this positioning would exhaust the sub-probe's available maneuvering power reserves in less than one Earth year. Repeated long-range scans of the second planet and its gravitational relationships with the other two planets were unable to yield a safe, practical orbital insertion plan for the sub-probe. As only two of the onboard mini-probes have self-adjusting maneuvering thrusters, the sub-probe determined it to be too great a risk to dispatch either one of them to investigate the second planet until more was understood about its planetary gravitational relationships and the debris field being created by the third planet. That being determined, the sub-probe reprogrammed one of its smallest and least sophisticated orbital mini-probes with the specific mission objective of gathering and relaying as much information as possible regarding the gravitational and debris fields located within the gravity well of the second planet.

Upon completing its programming, the sub-probe dispatched the mini-probe to the second planet via a trajectory passing it over the polar region of the third planet following a path parallel to the debris field between the second and third planets for as long as possible, before altering its trajectory to facilitate its proper orbital insertion around the second planet. As was the concern, during its first orbit of the second planet, the mini-probe was destroyed as it traversed the debris field. However, prior to its destruction, the mini-probe transmitted a wealth of critical data regarding the gravitational fields affecting the second planet, which the sub-probe's long-range scans were unable to detect. Upon altering its trajectory for orbital insertion around the second planet, the mini-probe's scans detected a null zone within the second planet's gravity well located between the second and third planet in direct alignment with the three planet's orbital plane. All simulations run by the sub-probe indicated that the sub-probe should be able to park itself in a stationery satellite orbital position within the null zone and remain in that position utilizing little to none of its power reserves.

While all simulations confirmed the sub-probe would be able to establish a stationery satellite orbital positioning within the discovered null zone, the sub-probe's self-preservation protocols elected to first attempt to park one of its two available self-maneuvering mini-probes in the null zone to ensure the accuracy of the flight trajectory and stationery satellite orbit positioning parameters being recommended by the simulations. Upon completing the mini-probe's programming the sub-probe dispatched the mini-probe, once again utilizing a trajectory passing it over the polar region of the third planet following a path parallel to the debris field between the second and third planets until altering its trajectory to initiate its all-stop orbital satellite parking maneuver. The release, flight and parking maneuver of the mini-probe was a flawless success and upon achieving its all-stop positioning, initiated its initial long and short-range scans. The mini-probe's long-range bio-life scans confirmed the existence of bio-life on the surface of the planet, however, while from this satellite positioning the surface of the planet is within the range of the sub-probe's short-range scanners, it is beyond the range of the mini-probe's short-range scanners. The mini-probe's short-range scans did however detect and confirm that the null zone was larger and more stable than as was reported by the initial orbital mini-probe. The mini-probe's long-range scans were also able to intercept communication transmissions in much greater detail and began a steady data stream of them to the sub-probe's linguistic compilers for interpretation and translation.

When the sub-probe completed its evaluation of the flight data of the now parked mini-probe, it calculated the necessary flight adjustments to compensate for the difference in its size and mass and embarked to rendezvous with the mini-probe. Just like the mini-probe, the sub-probe's flight and satellite positioning parking maneuver transpired flawlessly. Upon achieving its all-stop positioning the sub-probe began all initial long and short-range scans. As predicted by the simulations, the sub-probe is indeed able to maintain its stationery satellite positioning within the null zone utilizing little to none of its power reserves. Short-range scans indicate that the null zone is a gravitational magnetic void being maintained by the opposite polarities of the gravity wells of the second and third planets.

The sub-probe's short-range bio-life scans have confirmed the intermittent bio-life on the surface of the planet to be a bi-pedal humanoid species very similar in physiology and stature to that of humankind. Thus far, no other form of bio-life has been detected nor has any type of vegetation whatsoever been detected anywhere on the surface of the planet. The sub-probe's onboard linguistic compilers continue to evaluate this world's language structure based upon an extraordinarily high volume of intercepted communication transmissions, all of which are being sent to communication devices either being carried or worn by the humanoid species on the surface of the planet. Based upon the linguistic compilers translations thus far, it has been determined that the name given to this world by the inhabitants of the planet is Teti. Also, by the lack of any transmissions detected directed off world, the inhabitants of Teti appear to be unaware of the existence of life outside of their own world. Upon completing all of its initial scans, the sub-probe also confirmed there is no satellite technology in orbit around the planet and based upon all scientific data acquired from the intercepted transmissions thus far, the inhabitants have no space flight capabilities of any kind, nor have any references been made towards any kind of space exploration whatsoever.

The inhabitants of the planet Teti have been observed entering and exiting domed, hut-like structures, constructed of materials similar in molecular composition to that of bronze found on planet Earth. The extreme density of this bronze-like material makes these structures impervious to the meteorites that shower the planet's surface throughout its daily cycle. Due to these meteor showers, the inhabitants spend extremely limited periods of time on the planet's surface. Thus far, no other structures or apparent technology have been located on the planet's surface, subsequently, how these domed structures were constructed are as of yet unknown. It is speculated that these structures may be access points to an interconnected underground world. Also, due to the extreme density of the bronze-like material, none of the sub-probe's scans have been able to penetrate the structures, so the number of inhabitants or the technology they each contain is also as of yet unknown. Thus far, due to the unusual molecular composition of the rocky surface of the planet, the sub-probe's ground penetrating radar scans have only been able to detect sporadic traces of the bronze-like material below the surface in areas located between the detected clusters of huts, however, sufficient traces have been detected which has led to the speculation that not only are the hut clusters interconnected, but due to the number of inhabitants that have been detected on the surface, larger habitat structures of some kind must also exist underground. As thus far all indications are that the inhabitants are unaware of life outside of their own world, until more is known and understood about their underground activity and technology, the sub-probe will suspend first contact and landing a mini-probe on the surface. The sub-probe will continue to monitor the communication transmissions and will utilize the currently parked maneuverable mini-probe to make a closer flyover of the planet's surface to see if the mini-probe's short-range scanners will be able to learn more about the underground activity and the technological capabilities of the inhabitants of Teti.

.13
Bunker Dome In Boulder Valley

Probe Evad detected a trinary star system emitting high-frequency radio signals. Due to probe Evad's extensive distance from the system, while its long-range scans were able to detect planetary movement within the system, they were unable to determine the exact number of planets. Probe Evad's supplemental long-range scans were however able to confirm that one of the three stars was centrally located within the system and the other two stars were maintaining a tandem elliptical orbit around the central star. The supplemental scans also detected an asteroid belt orbiting the central star in an unusual orbital plane, at a nearly perfect 45° angle to that of the tandem star's orbital plane. Due to the structured constructs of the detected radio signals, probe Evad speculated that the likelihood of intelligent life existing within this system was high, so it fabricated and dispatched a Level 3 sub-probe to investigate. Also, due to the high probability for the existence of intelligent life, probe Evad enhanced the sub-probe's linguistic compilers and their data storage capacities, as well as fabricated and equipped the sub-probe with two additional self-maneuvering mini-probes.

As the sub-probe arrived at the system, it parked itself within the perimeter of the gravity well of the two stars orbiting the outer reaches of the system in tandem. Being parked in this position, the sub-probe was being gravitationally towed along the orbital plane by the tandem stars as they orbited the central star, allowing the sub-probe to use very little of its propulsion power reserves. These two tandem stars are nearly identical in size and mass and traverse their orbital plane locked in a gravitational anomaly causing them to continually revolve around one another. As the two stars rotate upon their individual axes, their gravitational forces continually draw upon one another causing them to revolve around one another, which this, along with the gravitational forces of the much larger central star, is what is maintaining their tandem orbital path around the central star. The sub-probe's long-range scans have detected eleven planets in orbit around the central star. Between the orbital paths of the eleventh planet and the tandem stars is an enormous asteroid belt nearly 280 million kilometers in width containing a countless number of asteroids and thousands of dwarf planets. All eleven planets are maintaining a near circular orbit around the central star. The sub-probe's long-range bio-life scans have detected a high concentration of bio-life on the ninth planet and a small concentration of bio-life on the tenth planet. While the ninth and tenth planets are just over 140 million kilometers apart from one another, their orbital speeds, along their respective orbital paths around the central star, are such that they maintain an almost identical alignment with one another and the central star, making the tenth planet a constant fixture in the night skies of the ninth planet. While numerous forms of vegetation have been detected on the sixth planet, along with signs of primitive animal life, the only signs of intelligent bio-life detected within this system is that which is located on the ninth and tenth planets.

The sub-probe's long-range scans detected several dozen technology-based satellites in orbit around the ninth planet and four in orbit around the tenth. Extremely limited spacecraft activity has been observed thus far, which is similar to that of Earth's early 21st century. The only spacecraft activity observed within the system has been a small number of flights between the ninth and tenth planets. Also, no spacecraft of any kind have been observed entering or exiting the system. While the sub-probe's long-range scans continue to detect the high-frequency radio signals as originally detected by probe Evad, due to magnetic interference being generated by the enormous asteroid field, from its orbital location along the tandem star's orbital path the sub-probe's linguistic compilers have been unable to identify or assemble any communication constructs from the signals. As the eleventh planet was then within 30° of the orbital alignment of the ninth and tenth planets, the sub-probe plotted a course to circumvent the asteroid field and insert itself in orbit around this planet. The sub-probe speculated that due to the limited technology that its long-range scans had detected and the distance the eleventh planet was from the ninth and tenth planets, that it could insert itself into orbit around the eleventh planet without risking accidental first contact with the inhabitants of the two planets. Upon completing the simulations of its proposed course and the trajectory chosen to circumvent the asteroid field and then realign itself for the orbital insertion maneuver, the sub-probe engaged its engines and embarked for the eleventh planet.

Due to the magnetic interference and a multitude of gravitational anomalies taking place within the asteroid field, while circumventing the field, the sub-probe was pushed thousands of kilometers off course. Once beyond the asteroid field's gravitational influences, the sub-probe had to make extensive course corrections, as the effects of the asteroid field had made the orbital insertion of the eleventh planet based upon the original plotted trajectory no longer possible. Rather than approaching the planet from behind within its orbital path and utilizing the planet's gravity well to draw it into orbit, the sub-probe now had to maneuver itself out in front of the planet within its orbital path and power its way into the planet's gravity well in a capture attempt orbital insertion. Not only would this maneuver require the sub-probe to use more of its propulsion power reserves, but also presented the possibility, due to the much greater planet approach velocity, of the sub-probe either skipping off the planet's gravity well, or entering the planet's gravity well at too sharp of an angle and crashing into the planet's surface. If the sub-probe were to skip off the planet's gravity well, the gravitational effect would cause the sub-probe's velocity to nearly double and would put it on a collision trajectory with the asteroid field. The sub-probe's simulations determined that at that velocity, to alter its trajectory and prevent itself from being destroyed within the asteroid field, it would exhaust all of its propulsion reserves in the attempt and would invariably drift into and be destroyed within the field. Along with the danger of potentially crashing into the planet's surface due to the planet's strong gravitational pull, should the sub-probe enter its gravity well at too sharp of an angle, once beyond the magnetic interference of the asteroid field, the sub-probe's short-range scans also detected high concentrations of extremely volatile methane in the planet's atmosphere, which several of the sub-probe's simulations indicated the potential of being ignited by the friction of the sub-probe's entry into it. As the potential for igniting the planet's atmosphere was not determined prior to the sub-probe entering the planet's gravity well, it was beyond the point of being able to abort the orbital insertion attempt. Due to this additional danger, the sub-probe made some last minute course corrections to minimize, as much as possible, the potential of igniting the atmosphere. As the sub-probe now had to power its way into orbital insertion, the sub-probe's engine would release a large volume of ion-plasma exhaust during the maneuver. There was insufficient time for the sub-probe to run any simulations to determine what effect if any, this large release of ion-plasma exhaust would have upon the planet's atmosphere.

The last minute course corrections made during planet approach turned out to be more critical than originally speculated. At the moment of orbital insertion when the sub-probe increased engine power to initiate the insertion maneuver, the gravitational forces of the planet were still greater than anticipated and the sub-probe was drawn much deeper into the planet's atmosphere than was projected. This being the case required the sub-probe to remain at near full engine power much longer than originally programmed in order for it to climb back up to a stable orbital altitude. By doing so, as was a concern raised in several of the orbital insertion simulations that the sub-probe had run, the atmosphere of the planet was indeed ignited, only much differently than any of the simulations predicted. The combination of the friction generated by the sub-probe's entry into the planet's atmosphere and the large volume of ion-plasma exhaust that was released by the sub-probe's engine during the orbital insertion maneuver, when mixed with the volatile methane of the planet's atmosphere, ignited, rapidly encompassing the planet forming a brilliant blue ring of flaming plasma and methane that nearly destroyed the sub-probe. Fortunately, as the sub-probe began its ascent towards a higher stable orbital altitude during its first orbit of the planet, it was spared the brunt of the impact of the initial combustion event. Before the sub-probe had completed its second orbit of the planet, rather than the atmosphere itself being ignited as well, due to the combination of the turbulent high winds of the planet's upper atmosphere and the extremely cold temperature of the atmospheric methane, the ring of flaming plasma and methane was instead extinguished by it, first by being flash-frozen and then the frozen particles initially being dispersed throughout the planet's atmosphere when the frozen ring exploded in a spectacular singular simultaneous event.

Upon establishing its stable orbit around the planet, the sub-probe immediately began its long-range scans of the ninth and tenth planets, initially focusing on any and all apparent communication signals in an attempt to determine if the planetary events caused by the sub-probe establishing its orbit around this eleventh planet had been observed and/or if the sub-probe itself had been detected by any of the inhabitants. The sub-probe had determined that when the ring of flaming plasma and methane was flash-frozen, its mass was then so great, that the powerful gravitational forces of the planet is what then caused the ring to explosively shatter. The high winds of the planet's upper atmosphere in conjunction with the planet's gravity, rapidly dispersed the shattered ring debris and then created a debris and crater field on the surface of the planet nearly 100 kilometers wide encompassing the planet around its equator, comprised of the remaining ring debris and the subsequent impact debris as a result of the tens of thousands of planetary impacts of the ring debris. Upon the sub-probe's onboard linguistic compilers completion of their initial evaluation of the language structure based on the intercepted communication signals, the sub-probe determined that the name the inhabitants of the ninth planet had given to their world is Bowlvey. It also determined that the inhabitants were very early into their space travel endeavors, the tenth planet being their first off-world exploration. Based upon the communication signals translated thus far, the inhabitants have not yet officially named the tenth planet. The closest English translation to how the inhabitants refer to the tenth planet is, stationary sparkle. Long-range scans of the tenth planet have also now confirmed that the bio-life detected on its surface, is a small colony of the inhabitants from Bowlvey and the technology located on the surface of the planet, is the beginnings of their establishment of permanent inhabitance of the planet. The sub-probe has also confirmed that there are no Moons in orbit around either of the two planets.

The on-going monitoring of the communication signals and long-range scans of Bowlvey, as well as the tenth planet, have detected several telescope facilities on the surface of Bowlvey and have confirmed that one of the facilities detected and documented the planetary event of the eleventh planet caused by the sub-probe. However, thus far, it appears that while the event itself was observed, due to the distance the eleventh planet is from Bowlvey, the telescopes are not powerful enough to have detected the sub-probe. Since the observance of the planetary event caused by the sub-probe, a multitude of transmissions have been detected indicating the inhabitants are now in the planning stages of dispatching a satellite to orbit and explore the eleventh planet. While the eighth planet is just slightly further from the ninth planet than is the tenth, due to the type of optics used in their telescopes and the brightness of this system's central star, the inhabitants of Bowlvey are unaware of the existence of any of the first eight planets of this system and believe their planet to be the closest world to their central star. The sub-probe also determined that the current orbital cycle of the eighth and ninth planets, would, for a limited time, put the two planets within range of the sub-probe's short-range scanners. As all indications are that the inhabitants of Bowlvey are unaware of life outside of their own world and the fact that they are now planning to send an exploratory satellite to this eleventh planet, to avoid the possibility of accidental first contact, the sub-probe has run a series of simulations towards establishing an orbit around the eighth planet.

After evaluating all of the simulations, the sub-probe selected an arched course relative to the planetary orbital plane, which will keep the sub-probe outside of the determined range of the Bowlvey telescopes. To minimize the amount of its propulsion power reserve usage, due to the planet approach course chosen, the sub-probe will enter the gravity well of the eighth planet perpendicular to its orbital plane, subsequently, the sub-probe will establish a polar orbit around the eighth planet. Prior to embarking for the eighth planet, the sub-probe initiated a final series of short-range scans of the eleventh planet, as well as a final series of long-range scans of Bowlvey and the tenth planet, while continuing to monitor communication transmissions between the two planets. As the eleventh planet was now regularly being observed by the telescope facilities on Bowlvey while their colony on the tenth planet was out of view during the rotational cycle of the tenth planet, to minimize the potential of being observed leaving orbit, the sub-probe programmed its departure from the eleventh planet and the course engagement for the eighth planet, to take place during the cycle when the colony on the tenth planet was back within view of Bowlvey and the telescope facilities were once again focused on the colony activities. When the sub-probe completed this final series of scans, it set course and as programmed, when the colony was back within view of Bowlvey, upon intercepting transmissions between the telescope facilities and the colony that their visual link had been re-established, the sub-probe engaged its engines leaving orbit of the eleventh planet and embarked for the eighth planet.

As per the simulations run by the sub-probe, the orbital insertion around the eighth planet transpired flawlessly. Short-range scans of the planet confirmed the planet to be void of any form of bio-life. Roughly twice the size of planet Earth, the planet is primarily composed of solid rock with a small solid iron core, which, in conjunction with its very slow rotation, produces an extremely weak planetary gravitational field. Initial short-range scans have also confirmed that the planet has no detectable atmosphere and its surface is heavily cratered and littered with impact ejecta rubble. As anticipated, due to the current planetary orbital positions, Bowlvey was now also currently within the sub-probe's short-range scanners range. Upon completing its initial scans of the eighth planet, the sub-probe initiated its comprehensive short-range scans of Bowlvey.

The planet Bowlvey, which is 858 kilometers less than three times the diameter of the planet Earth, surprisingly, has gravity almost identical to that of the Earth. The planet completes a single rotation in 70.1 Earth hours. Its atmosphere and weather patterns are also very similar to that of the planet Earth, the only significant difference being Bowlvey's atmosphere contains nearly four times the amount of Argon. The surface of the planet is made up of nearly equal proportions of land and liquid water, which is also almost identical in composition to the water found on planet Earth, the only significant difference being that thus far, based upon the sub-probe's initial scans, all of the water on the surface of the planet is equivalent to the fresh water of planet Earth and no salt water, like that of Earth's oceans, has as of yet been detected. The planet Bowlvey is heavily populated, with approximately twice the planetary population of that of the planet Earth, with a bi-pedal humanoid species similar in stature to humankind, with the exception of their average height of five meters. Based upon the sub-probe's initial scans, the inhabitants of Bowlvey appear to consist of three genders, male, female and a form of a hybrid of the two. Based upon the sub-probe's onboard linguistic compilers initial evaluation of Bowlvey's language structure from the intercepted communication transmissions, it is this hybrid being, that is responsible for propagating their species.

While the inhabitants of Bowlvey are in the early stages of their space exploration endeavors, they are a highly advanced technological species. Their world is powered by hundreds of thousands of small, interconnected reactor facilities, employing technology that thus far, the sub-probe is unable to comprehend. These facilities, as well as all of the industrial, commercial and residential facilities that have been scanned thus far, generate little to no detectable pollutants. The only emissions detected thus far being generated by their facilities and modes of transportation are minute traces of Argon, which explains the higher concentrations of it in the planet's atmosphere as compared to planet Earth. The inhabitants utilize a multitude of surface-based forms of transportation on both land and water, however, surprisingly, while the inhabitants have begun space travel endeavors, no form of any kind of air transportation has been detected thus far. Based upon the sub-probe's linguistic compilers translations of the intercepted transmissions thus far, this species is highly intelligent and insatiably dedicated to scientific research.

The inhabitants of the planet Bowlvey have completed construction of their Bunker Dome Research Facility. The facility was built in the approximate center of the mountain range located on the east coast of the planet's largest landmass. The facility was built to study the enormous boulders located in the main valley of the mountain range, some of which are almost as large as the facility itself, which is home to almost 4,000 research and support personnel. The facility's mission directive is to determine the origin and possible planetary significance of these enormous boulders. Unexpectedly, the sub-probe's initial scans of the planet's land surface, as well as its radar scans of the planet's surface beneath the planet's bodies of water, found no volcanic dome remnants anywhere on the planet. The sub-probe's evaluation of the enormous boulders based upon its initial surface scans has also determined that they are too large and dense to be the equivalent of glacier activity drop stones. Thus far, as is the case with the inhabitants of Bowlvey, the sub-probe has been unable to definitively determine the origin or the planetary significance, if any, of these enormous boulders.

Due to the high level of intelligence and technological advancement of the inhabitants of Bowlvey, they are deemed to be strong candidates for contact. The sub-probe has begun high-level secondary scans of the planet and has temporarily shut down all non-essential systems, so as to allocate as much power and computational resources as possible to its transmission detectors and linguistic compilers, towards learning as much as possible, as quickly as possible, about the inhabitants while the eighth planet remains within the sub-probe's scanners range of the planet Bowlvey. Simultaneously, the sub-probe will also continue to run simulations towards plotting an optimal course for the orbital insertion of Bowlvey when the appropriate time for contact has been established.

14

A Perimeter Marker In The Forest Of Greethum

Probe Evad's long-range scans detected some unusual readings in conjunction with apparent structured transmissions and faint signs of bio-life within a binary star system. Enhanced scans also detected four planets within the system, three of which are orbiting around one star, while the fourth is in orbit around the other. The enhanced scans also revealed both stars to be nearly identical in size, mass and composition. Due to probe Evad's distance from the system at the time of detection, it was unable to determine which planet or planets the signals were emanating from. As there was apparent structure to the transmissions and it was unable to identify the source or a purpose construct of the unusual readings detected within the system, probe Evad fabricated and dispatched a Level 3 sub-probe to investigate.

When the sub-probe reached its long-range scanner capable range of the system, it activated its first contact observational protocols and engaged its propulsion system to de-accelerate to its all-stop initial observational satellite position. The sub-probe's initial long-range scans of the system confirmed probe Evad's findings in that this system does indeed contain only four planets, three of which maintain close circular orbits around one of the binary stars, while the fourth planet orbits the second star just shy of being equidistant between the two stars. The sub-probe's initial long-range scans also determined that all of the detected transmissions and signals are originating from the single orbiting planet. The long-range scans also detected high concentrations of bio-life signs on the single planet, as well as determined the other three planets to be relatively featureless barren worlds. The sub-probe's enhanced secondary long-range scans detected no Moons in orbit around any of the three orbiting planets, nor was any discernible atmosphere detected around any of them. In orbit around the single orbiting planet, is a ring of debris speculated to be the remnants of the planet's Moon or Moons, that may have been destroyed by the opposing gravitational forces as the planet travels between the two stars during its orbital cycle. Thus far, it is speculated that the ring of debris is either the remnants of the destruction of this planet's Moon or Moons, or, due to the unusual gravitational forces that take place as the planet's orbit travels between the two stars, these forces are preventing a Moon or Moons from forming, as there are no indications that the debris is currently in any kind of coalescing process. Upon confirming that the three orbiting planets are void of any known form of bio-life, the sub-probe focused all of its enhanced long-range scans on the single planet.

The final round of enhanced long-range scans detected extremely high concentrations of bio-life on the surface of the planet. The planet is roughly 1.4 times the size of planet

Earth, and while signs of liquid water were detected on the planet's surface, the sub-probe's enhanced long-range scans were unable to detect any large bodies of water, such as oceans or lakes, nor were any major river systems detected. No technology based satellites were detected in orbit around the planet, nor were any spacecraft of any kind detected anywhere within this binary star system. From its current satellite positioning, the sub-probe was too far from the planet to be able to definitively identify the level of sophistication of the technology located on the planet's surface. Due to its current distance from the planet, the sub-probe was also unable to determine any language structures based upon the apparent communication transmissions, as its onboard linguistic compilers were unable to filter out the interference being caused by the additional unusual readings emanating from the planet. Upon completing its final round of long-range scans, the sub-probe, in order to minimize the potential of being detected, chose to orbit the planet just beyond the planet's debris ring, which would then also put the planet well within all of the sub-probe's short-range scanners range. When the sub-probe completed its final trajectory calculations and flight simulations, it engaged its engine and embarked for the planet.

Once the sub-probe established its stable orbit of the planet, it first performed extensive short-range scans of the planet's debris ring. As with the sub-probe's long-range scans, no signs of any of the debris coalescing were detected. The debris ranges in size from a few meters, to several hundred meters in diameter, yet surprisingly, very little small particle or dust debris is present anywhere within the orbiting debris ring. Also unusual, is the extremely slow rate of speed in which the debris ring orbits the planet. No bio-life signs of any kind, or water in any form were detected within the debris ring. Upon completing its scans of the debris ring, the sub-probe began its initial short-range scans of the planet. Unlike its long-range scans, the sub-probe's initial short-range scans were able to filter out the interference being caused by the unusual readings emanating from the surface of the planet and clearly identified that the readings were technology based. The initial scans determined that the unusual readings were a series of some form of power surges being randomly generated from thousands of different locations across the surface of the planet, with the highest concentration of readings emanating from the planet's southern hemisphere. The initial short-range topographical scans were also now able to accurately test, evaluate and map the surface of the planet.

The planet's surface consists of three primary liquid water oceans, similar to the oceans of planet Earth, with the exception of their higher sulfur concentrations, and hundreds of independent landmasses primarily separated by narrow rivers and marshes. Thus far, no fresh water like that of the inland lakes of planet Earth have been detected, nor has any frozen water ice been found anywhere on the planet's surface. The polar regions of the planet, which are also the planet's two largest landmasses, are riddled with small, extremely active volcanic mounds that are also the primary mountain ranges of the planet's surface. The planet wobbles in a slow random cycle nearly 34° offset from its true poles as it orbits its star, creating extreme internal pressures at its polar regions perpetually generating the volcanic eruptions. Other than at the planet's poles, which are clearly the hottest regions of the planet's surface due to the volcanic eruptions, the overall average planetary temperature is nearly a consistent 30° C, making the planet, the Earth equivalent, of a tropical rainforest on a planetary scale. The torrential rains that inundate the planet's surface, as well as the overall atmosphere, like the liquid water of the planet's surface, contain high concentrations of sulfur. However, the sub-probe's atmospheric scans have detected an as of yet unknown element present in the atmosphere that appears to be breaking down the high volume of sulfur being ejected into the atmosphere by the polar volcanic eruptions. The sulfur concentrations within the planetary rain, the planet's bodies of water and on the land surface of the planet, are far less than the sub-probe's calculations estimate that they should be. Upon completing its initial short-range scans of the planet, the sub-probe began its enhanced scans of the planet's surface.

The enhanced bio-life scans have found the planet to be inhabited by an intelligent bi-pedal species that average three meters in height. The overall planetary population is roughly twice that of the planet Earth and the inhabitants are clustered in heavily populated areas centrally located on almost every landmass of the planet's surface with the exception of the planet's polar regions. The inhabitants have a yellowish-green reptilian-like skin and two upper body appendages. The bio-life scans have identified and the language compilers have confirmed, that the inhabitants are a dual gender species, with the female gender, on average, the larger and stronger of the two genders. The bio-life scans have also detected an enormous volume and diverse species of plant and animal life forms on the planet's surface. The sub-probe's onboard linguistic compilers, once its communication detection system was able to filter out the technological interference emanating from the planet's surface, were able to assemble this world's language constructs and have determined that the name given to this world by its inhabitants is Greethum. The sub-probe's enhanced technological scans have detected a varying mixture of technologies on the surface of the planet, from very basic primitive water-powered facilities to a multitude of extremely sophisticated sulfur fueled power plants that are interconnected to thousands of units located on every landmass on the surface, with the exception of the two polar regions.

The inhabitants have developed a methodology for extracting the sulfur from the water, creating an extremely hot burning fuel, that is then utilized to heat the purified water in hundreds of extremely sophisticated steam powered plants strategically located throughout the planet's surface. The process they have developed for extracting the sulfur from the water and then efficiently burning it under the extreme pressure and temperature contained within these facilities, releases less than one thousandth the amount of sulfur they extract back into the atmosphere, along with vast amounts of purified water vapor released as excess steam from the facilities exhaust towers. This discovery has helped to explain why the sulfur concentrations in the planet's atmosphere, rainfall and surface water as detected by the sub-probe's atmospheric scans, is less than the sub-probe has calculated that they should be as a result of the perpetual polar volcanic eruptions. Surprisingly, with the estimated power output generated by these facilities, other than supplying power to the thousands of interconnected structures scattered across the planet's surface, no apparent major industrial facilities have been detected. Upon completing its initial enhanced scans of the planet, the sub-probe began its secondary enhanced scans focusing on the planet's bio-life and technology, while monitoring and translating the planetary communications.

The sub-probe's secondary enhanced scans have determined that while an intelligent species, the inhabitants of the planet Greethum are a relatively primitive species. The majority of the apparent industrial and commercial facilities is powered by the many primitive water-driven structures and is supported primarily by the physical labors of the male inhabitants. The sub-probe's onboard linguistic compilers have completed their initial evaluation of this world's language structure based upon the intercepted planetary communication transmissions. The planet is governed on a planetary scale through cooperative committees of elder females, with each landmass governed by its own committee. Thus far, no one female has been identified as the leader of any of the landmasses.

Planetary communications is primarily a primitive radio signal based system, with the landmasses linked together via send and receive towers located atop the governing facilities that have been constructed and centrally located on each of the inhabited landmasses. As originally detected by the enhanced bio-scans, the inhabitants are clustered in heavily populated areas centrally located on every landmass, with the exception of the polar regions and oddly, only very limited animal bio-life signs have been detected within these populated areas. The majority of animal bio-life signs are isolated within the outer perimeters of the planet's landmasses and on the surface of, or within, the bodies of water that separate them. The enhanced technological scans of the planet's surface have found that the majority of the habitat structures are constructed from the basic raw materials of the planet's surface, the trees, rock and surface soils. The only resemblance of major industrial facilities are adjunct structures to the sulfur fueled power plants that produce a small variety of glass and metal materials, which are primarily used in the construction of the units located along the perimeters of all but the polar region landmasses. The technological scans have also identified, with the help of the sub-probe's linguistic compilers, small scientific research facilities that are also a part of the industrial adjunct structures. Thus far, like the governing committees, all of the inhabitants that have been identified as scientists and research personnel are female.

Upon completing its initial technological scans, as well as translating the isolated communications between the scientific research facilities, the heavy volume of communication transmissions and construction activity that had been taking place on the planet's southern-most landmass, made it possible for the sub-probe to determine the purpose of the interconnected units. The inhabitants of the planet Greethum have installed disintegration perimeter markers along the forest's edge of the planet's southern-most landmass in an attempt to contain the planet's most deadly animal, the fanged Greewols, which have been responsible for over 400,000 deaths over the planet's past three star cycles alone. Greethum scientists were able to program the perimeter markers with the molecular composition of the people of Greethum, rendering the perimeter markers harmless to its citizens, yet instantaneously lethal to the Greewols. The sub-probe has also now confirmed that these perimeter markers are the source of the power surges and unusual readings that are emanating from the surface of the planet, as were originally detected by the sub-probe's initial long-range scans. This discovery has now also explained the limited number of animal bio-life signs that have been detected within the populated areas of the landmasses.

The inhabitants of the planet Greethum are unaware of life outside of their own world. While the inhabitants are an intelligent species, they are a relatively primitive species and other than the perimeter markers, little to no other forms of high technology have been detected. Their only form of planetary communications is the primitive radio signal based system, that is linked together via the send and receive towers located atop the governing facilities. Thus far, their scientific research appears to be limited to only these two technologies. No form of mechanical modes of transportation have been detected, the inhabitants traverse the surface of the planet solely under their own power by walking, running or swimming. Some inhabitants have been detected running at speeds of nearly 100 kilometers per hour and have been detected swimming at speeds of almost 130 kilometers per hour. Due to their current level of development as a species, the sub-probe will remain in its current orbital position and continue to monitor and explore the planet Greethum, but no attempts will be made to make first contact with the inhabitants for some time to come.

15

Together Eternal

Probe Evad detected an unusual twin binary star system with an apparent planetary orbital plane located in between the two pairs of binary stars. Due to probe Evad's distance from the system and the fact that the potential orbital plane was only visible edge-on when it was detected, its long-range scans were unable to definitively identify any planets or even confirm if it was indeed an orbital plane. Long-range scans were also unable to detect a central star within the suspected orbital plane, which would then make this a five star system. While no central star could be detected, nor could any planets be definitively identified, long-range scans were clearly indicating that there was in fact an orbital plane between the two pairs of binary stars and that it was not just some type of stellar debris or nebula. As probe Evad had previously had great success fabricating, assembling and releasing a tandem Level 3 sub-probe configuration, it elected to do so again, however, it decided to add yet one more additional set of modifications.

As this system was so far from probe Evad, it elected to add two more complete engine and propulsion support systems, mounted to either side of the united tandem Level 3 sub-probes, giving this version of the tandem sub-probes four complete propulsion systems, doubling the tandem sub-probe's maximum speed, simultaneously cutting its travel time to the system in half. Due to the fact that the two additional propulsion support systems consisted of only an engine, its matter collectors and fuel-processing module, as they were to be mounted to and controlled by the two main Level 3 control systems, they had no independent control systems of their own. Subsequently, probe Evad fabricated a small robotic assembly unit that was used to guide the two additional propulsion systems into place and make the necessary exterior connections to the two main tandem Level 3 sub-probes. When the robotic assembly unit completed its required tasks, it docked itself to probe Evad's fabrication module adjacent to the sub-probe release bay door and powered itself down entering a stand-by mode, leaving it available for possible future use.

When probe Evad had completed all of its final system checks of the tandem sub-probe, it ran its final release and sub-probe flight trajectory simulations. During the final trajectory simulations, probe Evad determined that due to the distance the system was from probe Evad's flight trajectory at that time, the one extra Communication Relay Pod included with this tandem sub-probe would not be sufficient for relaying the tandem sub-probe's reports back to its main Communication Relay Pod, which would remain within the flight trajectory of probe Evad. The small robotic assembly unit was reactivated and probe Evad fabricated two more Communication Relay Pods, each attached to its own mounting and release module. As probe Evad fabricated and released the two additional

Communication Relay Pod assemblies, they were captured by the robotic assembly unit and guided into position, installing one on top of each of the two additional propulsion support systems. When the robotic assembly unit completed the installation of the second additional Communication Relay Pod assembly, it once again docked with probe Evad and powered itself down entering its stand-by mode. Probe Evad ran a final round of complete system diagnostics on the tandem sub-probe including confirming that the communication links between all of the Relay Pods had been established. Upon completing the system diagnostics, probe Evad then ran one final series of release and sub-probe flight trajectory simulations compensating for the additional distance probe Evad had traveled since it began the communication modifications to the tandem sub-probe. As all of the tandem sub-probe's systems were confirmed mission ready, probe Evad initiated the release sequence and the tandem sub-probe embarked for the targeted twin binary star system.

As calculated by probe Evad, the tandem sub-probe with its two additional propulsion systems achieved an extraordinary rate of speed, which required it to perform extensive calculations in order to determine when to implement its braking maneuver, to slow itself down in time so as not to overshoot the twin binary star system and to properly place itself into its initial targeted satellite observational position of the system. The tandem sub-probe came to an all-stop position 103,000 kilometers from the suspected orbital plane and 53° offset of it, providing the sub-probe's long-range scanners a full perspective view of the entire suspected plane. The sub-probe immediately ran complete system diagnostics, powered up all long and short-range operational systems and then initiated its initial long-range scans of the system.

The initial long-range scans of the system confirmed that the suspected orbital plane located between the two pair of binary stars is indeed a planetary system. The planetary system consists of 17 major planets with a very dim brown dwarf star at its center, which is roughly 82 times the mass of the planet Jupiter of planet Earth's solar system. While brown dwarf stars typically give off large amounts of infrared radiation, due in large part to this star's extremely minimal deuterium fusion, it has a very small infrared signature and a very low surface temperature, resulting in its nearly undetectable dull red color. Even with this star's slow gravitational contractions, its gravitational influences are sufficient enough to keep the 17 major planets, in conjunction with their combined gravitational fields, in a relatively consistent, slightly elliptical orbital plane around its central location. Much of the space in between the planetary orbital paths is littered with asteroids and spatial debris speculated to be remnants of this system's original circumstellar disk, which is clearly still in the process of multiple planetary accretions.

Long-range bio-life scans of the planetary system have detected bio-life signs on the fifth planet from the central brown dwarf star. Thus far, the only other bio-life signs that have been detected within the planetary system have been minimal readings in the immediate vicinity of the fifth planet, speculated to be located on the surface of one or more of the Moons in orbit around the planet as at the current distance the sub-probe is from the fifth planet, precise readings are not possible. The sub-probe's long-range technological scans have also only been able to detect faint signs of apparent high technology and potential signs of communication signals, however, again due to the sub-probe's current distance from the planet, as well as distortion being caused by the multiple gravitational fields of the remaining outer planets and the planetary accretion belts, precise readings are not possible. Upon completing its final series of enhanced long-range scans of the planetary system, as no other signs of bio-life or technology were detected within the system, nor were any signs of spacecraft activity detected leaving or entering the system, the sub-probe began running flight simulations towards formulating a slow, gradual approach to the fifth planet in order to minimize the potential for its detection, should the bio-life signs that have been detected on and within the vicinity of the fifth planet be that of intelligent life. When the sub-probe had established what it believed to be a safe trajectory towards the fifth planet while traversing the various gravitational fields of the outer planets and planetary accretion fields, it engaged two of its four engines and began its slow approach towards the fifth planet, while maintaining its continual enhanced long-range scans of the planet and its orbiting moons.

Upon traveling beyond the accretion field, which innermost boundary from the central star is located just 80,000 kilometers from the seventh planet of the system, the sub-probe's long-range scans were then able to detect and identify clear indications of structured communication signals emanating from the fifth planet. As at that point the detected signals were very strong, the sub-probe altered its programmed trajectory towards the fifth planet, instead, setting course for inserting itself into an orbit around the seventh planet, which required only minor course corrections as the seventh planet was in nearly perfect alignment with the fifth planet and the central star. Once a stable orbit was established around the seventh planet, the sub probe first initiated short-range scans of this planet.

The seventh planet is a gas giant roughly the size and mass of the planet Saturn of planet Earth's solar system. The atmosphere of the planet, also strikingly similar to the planet Saturn, is primarily composed of hydrogen, helium and small traces of methane. Initial scans of the planet did not detect any type of solid surface nor were any signs of bio-life or technology detected. The sub-probe also confirmed that oddly, for a planet of this size and mass, there are no Moons in orbit around it. While the short-range scans were underway of this planet, the sub-probe also completed its evaluation of its long and short-range scans that it performed on the outer 10 planets and three planetary accretion fields encountered while en route to this planet. All of the scans that were performed while en route confirmed the sub-probe's initial long-range scans of the system and no signs of bio-life or technology other than those detected on and within the vicinity of the fifth planet have been detected. When the sub-probe completed its short-range scans of this planet, it altered its orbit of the planet entering into a polar orbit perpendicular to the planet's orbital plane. This orientation of polar orbit gave the sub-probe an unobstructed long-range scanner view of the remaining inner planets and final planetary accretion field of this system. The remaining accretion field is located in between the second and third planets and the sub-probe's initial long range scans of the field indicate signs of three major planetary bodies being formed within this extremely dense field. Upon completing its enhanced long-range scans of the inner planets and remaining accretion field after reorienting its orbit around this seventh planet, the sub-probe was able to definitively confirm that the first four planets, as well as the sixth, were void of any type of bio-life and no signs of any form of technology of any kind was detected on, or within the vicinity of, any of these planets. While the extreme density of the accretion field located in between the second and third planets, in addition to the distance the sub-probe currently is from the field, makes it impossible to be 100% conclusive, there were also no signs indicating that any form of bio-life or technology was present anywhere within the field either. With this series of scans completed, the sub-probe now focused all of its systems on the fifth planet and began enhanced scans of it, as well as the Moons in orbit around it.

The fifth planet is just slightly larger than planet Earth, at 1.3 times its size and rotates once on its axis, which is tilted just 2° offset from its true magnetic poles, in just over 26 Earth hours. A total of six irregular shaped asteroid Moons have been detected in a relatively consistent equatorial orbital plane around the planet. The communication transmissions emanating from the fifth planet are extremely high-frequency electromagnetic signals similar to the microwave transmissions used on planet Earth. The major differences being that the signals emanating from the planet are much more focused data-streams with frequencies nearly seven times greater than the microwave signals utilized on the planet Earth. Due to the structure of the data-streams and the extremely high frequency at which they are being transmitted, the extraordinary volume of data being transmitted per data-stream had repeatedly overloaded the sub-probe's linguistic compilers. As the fifth planet was currently beyond the range of the sub-probe's short-range scanners, the sub-probe re-routed their main, as well as their sub-processing data systems, to assist the linguistic compilers with the exorbitant volume of data. While the volume of data was still greater than the linguistic compilers could process in real time even with the assistance of all of the short-range scanner systems, with the short-range scanner systems filtering and buffering the transmissions, they were then able to consistently stream the transmissions to the linguistic compilers at their maximum reception data rate, not only preventing the overloading of the linguistic compilers processing systems, but also finally allowing them to properly evaluate the transmissions and formulate this worlds language structure. Simultaneously, the sub-probe had completed its initial enhanced scans of the fifth planet and the Moons in orbit around it.

Based on the linguistic compiler's translations of the transmissions that have been evaluated thus far, the name given to this world by its inhabitants is Nalto. This world is inhabited by a bi-pedal humanoid species consisting of two genders, male and female. The inhabitants are physiologically similar to humankind except for their average stature being nearly four meters and their lack of any body hair of any kind. Also, thus far none of the inhabitants have been observed wearing any type of clothing or ornamental garments of any kind. Their skin is a light grey in color and other than the obvious gender differences there are very little differences in physical appearance between the inhabitants. While all indications, based upon the translations of the intercepted communications and enhanced scans completed thus far, are that the inhabitants of the planet Nalto are an extremely intelligent species, no references have been found to indicate that they are aware of any form of life outside of their own world. Based upon the data gathered and evaluated thus far no clear form of structured government or ruling leaders have been identified, nor have any type of conflicts between any of the inhabitants been detected anywhere on the surface of the planet. All indications thus far are that the inhabitants of Nalto are a peaceful and cooperative species on a planetary scale. There is little to no vegetation anywhere on the surface of the planet nor have any signs of liquid or frozen water been detected. The only liquid detected on the surface of the planet which also appears to be the only form of nourishment consumed by the inhabitants of the planet, is a thick murky grey liquid that slowly bubbles and erupts from small cone shaped structures that collects in small pools that encompass the structures. A countless number of these structures have been detected scattered across the entire surface of the planet and while relatively consistent in size, appear to be naturally formed structures as opposed to any form of technology developed by the inhabitants. Thus far no reference as to what the inhabitants call these structures or the liquid that they produce, which they in turn consume, has been found. Oddly, while the initial round of enhanced bio-life scans have clearly identified male and female genders amongst the inhabitants, no identifiable offspring have been detected anywhere on the planet's surface.

The sub-probe's evaluation of the initial round of enhanced long-range technological scans has yielded several unusual results as well. No signs of habitats, commercial or industrial structures of any kind have been detected on the surface of the planet. The only high technology detected on the surface of the planet is small spacecrafts capable of transporting eight inhabitants. These crafts have been observed transporting inhabitants to not only various locations on the planet's surface, but to several of the Moons orbiting the planet as well. Thus far the sub-probe has not been able to identify any source or technology related to how the communication transmissions are being transmitted. As no other high technology, other than the small spacecrafts, has been detected on the surface of the planet, nor have any kind of habitat structures of any kind been detected, the sub-probe can only presume that some form of underground network must exist below the surface of the planet. Due to the sub-probe's current distance from Nalto and the unusual composition of the planet's surface, the sub-probe is unable to scan beneath the surface. While the sub-probe speculates that some form of underground network must exist, thus far, none of the long-range scans have detected any locations for, nor observed any of the inhabitants, accessing an underground network from the surface of the planet. As several spacecrafts had been detected traveling to and from several of the Moons in orbit around the planet, the sub-probe began a series of enhanced long-range scans focused on the Moons and the spacecrafts in transit to them.

The spacecrafts while in transit to one of the Moons in orbit around the planet travel at considerably greater velocity than when they are shuttling inhabitants around on the surface of the planet. While in transit, as well as when they are on the surface of one of the Moons they are currently exploring, the inhabitants still wear no form of clothing or protective spacesuit of any kind. While humanoid and the long-range bio-life scans have confirmed that the inhabitants have nostrils, a mouth and lungs, it is as of yet unknown what it is that they breathe, as the sub-probe has detected no discernible atmosphere of any kind either on the surface of the planet Nalto, nor on any of the Moons in orbit around it. Thus far, no form of technology other than the spacecrafts has been detected on any of the planet's Moons. Based upon the transmissions that the sub-probe has evaluated thus far, the inhabitants are in the early stages of exploring the Moons in orbit of their world and there are currently only a small number of inhabitants on four of its six Moons. On one of the asteroid Moons of the planet Nalto two sculptures were discovered in an excavated shallow cave. As the sculptures were discovered during the first exploratory space flight and landing on the Moon by the inhabitants of the planet Nalto, the creators of the sculptures, or when they were created is unknown, as there are also no known references to the sculptures in the Nalto's recorded history. Inexplainably however, carved into the rock above the opening to the cave in the Nalto's native language is an inscription. The English translation of this inscription is "If love is true, it should last for eternity." It appears that this Moon was the first Moon that the inhabitants explored and that the discovery of these sculptures is what launched their exploratory efforts of the other Moons. Thus far all indications are that the inhabitants have not found any other statues, or any reference to them, on any of the other Moons they have explored thus far. Were it not for the intercepted transmissions, the sub-probe would never have detected the statues within the cave as from the distance the sub-probe currently is from the Moon, the statues are indiscernible from the surrounding rock of the cave. Transmissions that have been intercepted not only reference exploring the remaining two Moons but references have also been detected that indicate the inhabitants are planning to explore the sixth planet as well.

As the sub-probe has not been able to detect any technology on the planet Nalto other than the small spacecrafts, it is as of yet unknown how the inhabitants are even aware the sixth planet exists. Thus far, no mention of any of the other planets of the system has been detected, nor has any mention of the sub-probe being observed been detected. The sub-probe will continue to learn as much as it can about the inhabitants of the planet Nalto by continuing its monitoring and evaluation of the transmissions emanating from the planet as well as the small spacecrafts. Until the sub-probe can better understand what the level of technological capabilities of the inhabitants of Nalto truly are, it will remain in its current orbit around this seventh planet and will suspend the launch of any mini-probes as well as postpone making first contact with this species.

.16
Copper Buoy

Probe Evad detected an unusual light-based signal emanating from a planet in an extraordinarily fast elliptical orbit around a pulsar star. As the radio wave interference being generated by the pulsar star was so great, probe Evad's long-range scans were unable to establish a definitive source or purpose of the light-based signal other than that the signal was originating from the surface of the single planet in orbit of the pulsar star. Probe Evad's long-range bio-life scans were also unable to detect any signs of bio-life on the planet. As the light-based signal was clearly identified as originating from the surface of the planet, probe Evad fabricated and dispatched a Level 2 sub-probe to investigate. Due to the intensity of the radio wave interference being generated by the pulsar star, probe Evad added additional shielding to the sub-probe's scanner systems to help minimize the effects and filter out as much of the radio wave interference as possible.

When the sub-probe reached its full scanner capable range, it activated its first contact observational protocols and engaged its propulsion system to de-accelerate to its all-stop initial observational satellite position. When the sub-probe established its all-stop positioning it initiated its long-range scans of the system. The pulsar star is a mere 17 kilometers in diameter but is nearly twice the mass of the Sun of planet Earth's solar system. The single planet in orbit around the star maintains an elliptical orbit bringing it within 53 million kilometers from the star at it closest point, to roughly 71 million kilometers at its furthest distance from the star. Remarkably, even at these distances from the pulsar star, the planet completes a single orbit around the star in roughly 192 Earth hours. The most unusual aspect of the planet's orbit is that due to the combination of the extreme gravitational forces of the pulsar star and the elliptical orbit the planet maintains, the planet does not completely rotate on its axis. Instead, the rotation of the planet changes directions vacillating back and forth on its axis as it orbits the star, an orbital phenomenon never observed before. Due to its elliptical orbit, at its furthest distance from the star, the planet reaches a rotational positioning of nearly 190° before reversing direction, resulting in the entire surface of the planet being exposed to the light and radiation of the pulsar star at some point during its orbit. It is also when the planet is at its closest and furthest distances from the star, that the planet's rotational direction is reversed and the light-based signal is being generated. This orbital phenomenon results in the planet's unusual daily cycle of the pulsar star rising and setting from the same horizon on an alternating horizon basis, which in turn, generates the light-based signal from the surface of the planet four times during each orbit of the pulsar star.

The sub-probe's initial, as well as enhanced long-range scans, confirmed probe Evad's findings and found no signs of bio-life of any kind on the surface of the planet. While the sub-probe's long-range technological scans confirmed the light-based signal was indeed originating from the surface of the planet, they were unable to identify any type of technology responsible for generating the signal. As the sub-probe had determined it had gathered as much data about the planet as it could from its current distance from it and by utilizing only its long-range scanners, the sub-probe began running flight simulations towards positioning itself within its short-range scanner range of the planet. Based upon its initial simulations, the combination of the incredible speed in which the planet orbits the pulsar star and the unusual alternating gravitational fields of the planet, in conjunction with the extremely powerful gravitational fields generated by the pulsar star, staying within short-range scanner range of the planet by orbiting the planet would not be possible. Further simulations led to the sub-probe's discovery of a gravitational null zone located above the planetary orbital plane within the pulsar star's northern pole's rotational ring. This location would place the sub-probe in a position outside of the pulsar star's magnetic field lines, as well as out of any direct alignment with the pulsar star's northern emission beam. The major concern identified by the sub-probe's simulations with establishing this satellite positioning was that to do so, due to the extremely rapid rotation of the pulsar star, the sub-probe would have to endure a brief direct alignment exposure to the pulsar star's northern emission beam. As the amount of electromagnetic radiation contained in the emission beams being generated by the pulsar star is beyond the sub-probe's capacity to calculate, the sub-probe could only speculate the potential damage even a brief exposure to this intensity of electromagnetic radiation could cause to its operational systems. Upon completing its review of all of the flight simulations it had run towards establishing a satellite positioning that would allow the sub-probe to maintain short-range scanner capability of the planet, as well as put the planet within control range of its onboard mini-probes, its only option was to attempt to insert itself into the gravitational null zone 715,858 kilometers above the planetary orbital plane placing it within the pulsar star's northern pole's rotational ring, as every alternative simulation resulted in the assured destruction of the sub-probe. With its decision made, the sub-probe ran extensive flight simulations focusing on alternative trajectories for inserting itself into the target null zone and minimizing its exposure to the pulsar star's emission beam's electromagnetic radiation.

As the sub-probe was incapable of definitively calculating the effect the electromagnetic radiation of the pulsar star's emission beam would have on its operational systems, the sub-probe formulated a sequence for the shutting down of all non-essential systems during the insertion maneuver. While probe Evad had equipped the sub-probe with additional shielding to protect the sub-probe's scanner systems from the excess radio wave interference that it had first detected, the sub-probe speculated the additional shielding would be insufficient to fully protect them from the electromagnetic radiation of the pulsar star's emission beam. It was also a major concern what effect the incalculable associated electromagnetic pulse would have on its propulsion and related systems. Based upon the initial insertion trajectory simulations, one of the most critical steps of the insertion maneuver sequence would be achieving the all-stop positioning within the pulsar star's northern pole's rotational ring. The sub-probe had determined that if it were to shut down all of its propulsion related systems in an attempt to protect them from the emission beam during the insertion maneuver, due to the momentum the sub-probe would achieve during the maneuver, there would be insufficient time to restart the propulsion systems and initiate the braking sequence in order to achieve its all-stop positioning within the gravitational null zone. Subsequently, as shutting down any of the propulsion related systems was not an option, the sub-probe ran a multitude of simulations towards formulating alternatives for protecting these critical systems.

The sub-probe finally determined that by utilizing its outbound communication signaling system in conjunction with its engine power control system, it could generate an electromagnetic pulse of its own. Multiple simulations based upon the sub-probe's speculated strength of the electromagnetic pulse and radiation of the pulsar star's emission beam, indicated that the electromagnetic pulse the sub-probe could generate would temporarily envelop the sub-probe in an electromagnetic bubble, that would then disperse the pulsar star's emission beam's electromagnetic pulse and radiation around the sub-probe. This sequence would have to be precisely timed and initiated so as to coincide with the 2.8 seconds it would take the sub-probe to cross the pulsar star's northern rotational ring while enduring the repeated pulses of the emission beam. Upon completing its evaluation of all of the flight trajectory simulations and making its final decision choosing this scenario, which would give it not only as much time as possible to reengage its propulsion systems and initiate the braking maneuver, but would also ensure that it cross the pulsar star's northern rotational ring in just 2.8 seconds subjecting it to as few of the pulsar star's emission beam's electromagnetic pulses and as little of its incalculable radiation as possible, the sub-probe began the programming of this extremely complicated sequence. When the sub-probe had completed the programming, it ran a final complete series of simulations including the powering down, as well as the subsequent re-initialization and power-up sequences of all of its systems, to confirm its time estimates for this complicated series of tasks could indeed be completed within the estimated timeframes. As a number of simulations resulted in the sub-probe being destroyed during this insertion maneuver, the sub-probe relayed all of the data it had compiled about this pulsar star system, along with all of the flight simulation scenarios it had performed regarding the insertion maneuver chosen to its Communication Relay Pod. When the data relay was complete, the sub-probe engaged its engine and initiated the insertion maneuver sequence embarking for its target location.

While en route to its target location the sub-probe detected ultra-high-speed radio wave signals emanating from a previously undetected planetary system located spatially above the orbital plane of this pulsar star system. While being transmitted at ultra-high-speed, the structure of the transmission signals consisted of extremely rudimentary binary language constructs. As its communication and linguistic compiler systems were to be the last systems to be shut down during the insertion maneuver and no other tasks, other than those that were required to implement the maneuver had been scheduled, the sub-probe began compiling and evaluating the transmission signals. As the sub-probe's long range bio-life scans had detected no bio-life on the surface of the planet, just prior to shutting down its mini-probe dispatch systems in preparation for the insertion maneuver, as the planet was then within orbital insertion range of the mini-probe's, the sub-probe released a series of mini-probe's targeted to orbit and explore the planet. Just as the sub-probe was about to begin the power-down sequence of its long-range scanner systems, the long-range scanners detected an enormous object traveling at nearly the speed of light, originating from the planetary system that was transmitting the binary signals and was heading directly for this pulsar star system. Unfortunately, as the time had come to power-down the long-range scanners as per the programmed sequence of the insertion maneuver, other than determining that the object was a high-technology-based spacecraft of some kind, there was insufficient time to gather or compile any further data regarding the craft. Within minutes of the final mini-probe transmitting its successful orbital insertion data to the sub-probe, which then confirmed that all of the mini-probes that the sub-probe had dispatched to the planet had indeed been successfully inserted into orbit of it, the sub-probe initiated its final short-range scans of the pulsar star and its target location, confirming it was still precisely on course. Prior to shutting down the linguistic compilers as scheduled for the insertion maneuver, the sub-probe had determined, based upon the translations of the transmission signals it had completed thus far, that the name given to the planet in orbit around the pulsar star is Yellwatclur. While the detected transmission signals consist of extremely rudimentary binary language constructs, the enormous volume of raw data they contain will require a considerable amount of time to fully translate and evaluate. Once again, to preserve the data the sub-probe had gathered and compiled from the transmission signals, as well as the short-range scans of the pulsar star and planet that it was able to complete, should the sub-probe be damaged or destroyed during the insertion maneuver, the sub-probe transmitted a back up of the data to its Communication Relay Pod. As scheduled, when the sub-probe reached its programmed distance from the pulsar star's northern rotational ring, it powered down all of its systems, with the exception of its outbound communication signaling system and its engine power control system. When the final system confirmed it had been powered down, the entry segment of the insertion maneuver program was initiated beginning the sub-probe's final flight phase towards establishing its target location.

As per the multitude of simulations it had run, the electromagnetic bubble the sub-probe was able to generate was indeed successful at dispersing the majority of the pulsar star's emission beam's electromagnetic pulses and radiation around the sub-probe, however, the bubble was not strong enough to withstand the extraordinary intensity of the radiation, in combination with the repeated impacts of the pulsar star's emission beam, in their entirety. The sub-probe's engine was damaged due to the direct exposure to the electromagnetic pulses and radiation of the emission beam and when the sub probe's propulsion system engaged the engine to initiate the braking maneuver required for the sub-probe to achieve its all-stop position, a catastrophic fusion fuel system chain reaction failure transpired causing the engine to explode. Miraculously, none of the sub-probe's other systems were damaged as a result of the explosion and due to the resulting shock wave generated by the explosion, in combination with the sub-probe's emergency activation of its maneuvering thrusters, the sub-probe was still able to achieve an all-stop positioning within the gravitational null zone within the pulsar star's northern pole's rotational ring, however, the sub-probe had not only overshot its targeted all-stop positioning by nearly 20,000 kilometers, but had also exhausted all but seconds of its available thruster fuel reserve, potentially stranding the sub-probe in its current location within the null zone. As per the pre-programming of the insertion maneuver, when the sub-probe had achieved an all-stop positioning, the re-activation sequence was initiated to bring all of the sub-probe's systems back on line. While the engine had been destroyed as a result of the explosion during the insertion maneuver, the sub-probe's system start-up diagnostics confirmed that all of the power generation systems were in tact and functioning at full capacity, which would maintain the operation of the sub-probe's scanner, communications and mini-probe control systems, however, the explosion had also damaged the fusion fuel production and storage systems, then confirming that the sub-probe was indeed stranded at its current all-stop location. Upon completing the start-up sequences of all of its available systems, the sub-probe began short-range scans of the planet Yellwatclur and reestablished communications links with the mini-probes it had placed into orbit around the planet prior to its insertion maneuver into this gravitational null zone. As the communications links with the mini-probes were reestablished, the sub-probe downloaded and evaluated all of the exploratory data gathered by the mini-probes.

Large pointed domes made of a material with similar reflectivity to that of polished copper found on planet Earth, were found floating, in stationery positions, in the unidentifiable crystal clear liquid that covers over one third of the planet Yellwatclur. None of the onboard scanners, sensors or mini-probes were able to penetrate the domes or determine their molecular composition. No known life forms were detected on the planet's surface. By the positioning of the 9 domes located, the speculation is that they are some kind of buoy markers, due to the convergence of light reflections that occur at dawn each day at the location of the domes. This convergence can only be seen from orbit at a distance of 237 kilometers or greater. The purpose of these buoys, or the light-convergence they create, is as of yet, unknown. The sub-probe's long-range scans had once again detected and has now confirmed, that the enormous spacecraft that the long-range scans detected just prior to initiating the insertion maneuver into this null zone, is indeed on a direct course for this pulsar star system and should arrive within short-range scanner range, as well as be within direct instantaneous communication range of the sub-probe, in approximately 68 Earth days.

As the sub-probe is currently stranded at its current all-stop position here in this gravitational null zone due to the damage it sustained during the insertion maneuver, its encounter and first contact with the spacecraft en route is inevitable. The sub-probe has amended its standard first contact communication data stream to include the pertinent information regarding its damaged state. As thus far no transmission signals have been detected from the spacecraft, the sub-probe's linguistic compilers will continue to evaluate the ultra-high-speed radio wave signals that continue to emanate from the planetary system the craft is en route from, in the attempt to translate and understand as much as possible about the language constructs so as to be as prepared as possible for its initial encounter with the spacecraft when it arrives. In the event that the intentions of the craft are hostile, the sub-probe will transmit a complete system data download to its Communication Relay Pod just prior to the craft reaching this system.

17

Deep Space Research Lab

Probe Evad detected a star cluster consisting of a multitude of planetary systems. As long-range scans detected a high volume of communication transmissions, as well as dense concentrations of varying forms of bio-life, probe Evad fabricated a Level 3 sub-probe to investigate. Due to the high volume of communication transmissions, probe Evad included a number of enhancements to the sub-probe's linguistic compilers and communication systems, including the addition of several external transponder dishes with reposition capabilities. Due to the size and exterior locations of these transponder dishes, they could not be assembled in position within probe Evad's fabrication module. To complete the assembly and addition of these transponder dishes, probe Evad had to reactivate the docked small robotic assembly unit and complete the fabrication of the sub-probe externally within the gravitational tow field. Upon completing the fabrication of the sub-probe, the robotic assembly unit returned to its docked position with probe Evad and powered itself down into standby mode. Probe Evad then ran complete system diagnostics on the sub-probe while the sub-probe simultaneously tested all of its transponder dish repositioning and communication relay systems. When all of the diagnostics were complete and all systems verified they were mission ready, probe Evad ran final trajectory calculations, uploaded the course corrections to the sub-probe and released it, initiating its mission to investigate the star cluster planetary systems.

While en route to the targeted star cluster, the sub-probe's long-range scans not only detected relatively consistently constructed communication transmissions in between the multitude of planetary systems, but also detected a high volume of spacecraft activity within, as well as in between, many of the planetary systems. While hundreds of diverse and unique language constructs have been detected, one in particular has been detected in use in every planetary system detected thus far and is the primary language construct that is being used for communication purposes by the spacecrafts that have been detected traversing throughout the planetary systems of the star cluster. Upon making this determination, the sub-probe focused its scans and linguistic compilers towards translating this dominant language construct while en route to the star cluster. Enhanced secondary long-range scans of the star cluster were finally able to definitively determine the closest star, which maintains a planetary system of five planets. While the enhanced scans detected signs of bio-life only on the fourth planet, only one spacecraft was detected within this planetary system and it was in orbit around the outermost fifth planet from this system's star. As this star and the planetary system it maintains was not only the closest system from the sub-probe's current location, but also appears to have the least amount of bio-life and technological activity of all of the systems that are a part of this targeted star cluster, the sub-probe began programming a new trajectory which would put it on course for an observational satellite position located outside of this system, but within its full long-range scanner capable range of the outermost fifth planet. When the new trajectory programming was completed and verified, the sub-probe initiated the new program and embarked for its newly selected target location.

While en route to the first targeted system, the sub-probe's linguistic compilers completed their initial evaluations and translations of the language constructs of the communication transmissions that are predominantly in use by the majority of the spacecrafts that have been detected traveling throughout the star cluster. Based upon these initial translations, the sub-probe has determined that the spacecraft in orbit around the fifth planet is from a nearby planetary system and is in orbit of the fifth planet for the purpose of monitoring the activities of the inhabitants of the fourth planet. The sub-probe has translated its first contact messages into the predominate language construct being used by the spacecrafts and has completed the preparation of its first contact transmission, which has now been buffered by its outbound communication system and is ready for immediate transmission. When the sub-probe reached its full long-range scanner capable range of the first targeted system, it activated its first contact observational protocols and engaged its propulsion system to de-accelerate to its all-stop initial observational satellite position. When the sub-probe had achieved its all-stop positioning, it initiated all power-up sequences for all of its long-range, as well as, its short-range scanner systems and performed complete system diagnostics of all systems as they acknowledged their mission-ready status. Upon completing all system diagnostics and confirming all systems were indeed fully functional, the sub-probe initiated its initial long-range scans of the fifth planet and the spacecraft in orbit of it.

Within seconds of the sub-probe initiating its long-range scans of the spacecraft, it left orbit of the fifth planet and traveled a direct course towards the location of the sub-probe. The sub-probe immediately began repeatedly transmitting its buffered translated first contact transmissions. The spacecraft traveled at an astonishing rate of speed, arriving at the sub-probe's location in a matter of minutes and coming to an all-stop position located just 48 meters from the sub-probe. While an object approaching this close to the sub-probe would normally auto-engage its defensive shielding and warning systems, as it was known the approaching object was a spacecraft and was apparently reacting to it first being scanned by the sub-probe, the sub-probe speculated these actions could be interpreted as a hostile posture and so, disengaged its defensive systems as it continued to repeatedly transmit its prepared first contact transmissions. Finally, after repeating its first contact transmissions nearly 100 times, the sub-probe received a short transmission from the spacecraft. The sub-probe immediately stopped sending its first contact transmissions and focused all of its resources on translating the spacecraft's transmission. The closest English translation the linguistic compilers could derive from the spacecraft's transmission was "hold location for evaluation". Moments after the linguistic compilers established this translation, simultaneously every system of the sub-probe entered the equivalent of their full diagnostic modes. Based upon the spacecraft's transmission, the sub-probe could only speculate that the craft was somehow responsible for the initiation of the diagnostics and that its systems were somehow being scanned and evaluated. Suddenly, the sub-probe experienced a system-wide power drain, comparable to a complete shut down and reboot of all of its systems, after which, the sub-probe was once again back in control of all of its systems and found itself in a tandem orbit with the spacecraft around the fifth planet. Just as the sub-probe was about to transmit its secondary first contact transmissions to the spacecraft, which included the sub-probe's detailed directives of its mission of peaceful exploration and its desire for the open exchange of information, as well as inquire about the spacecraft's apparent scans, evaluation and how and why the sub-probe was now here in orbit around the fifth planet, the sub-probe began receiving a transmission from the spacecraft being sent in perfectly translated English.

The spacecraft's transmission confirmed that it had indeed scanned all of the sub-probe's systems and has assimilated all of its on-board data and technology. The transmission also confirmed that the spacecraft was responsible for the temporary shut down of the sub-probe's systems, as it was deemed necessary to do so to prevent them from being damaged by the rapid acceleration and precise orbital insertion maneuver, in conjunction with the spacecraft's simultaneous implementation of an extremely powerful energy-based masking field, required to ensure that the spacecraft and sub-probe not be detected by the inhabitants of the fourth planet. The transmission included the notification, that due to the spacecraft's scan's detection of multiple heavily encrypted data files that they were unable to access and evaluate, as well as the spacecraft's inability to determine the origin of the sub-probe, that all of the data that had been collected as a result of its scans had been transmitted to its home world along with its request for official instructions as to how to continue its interaction with the sub-probe. The transmission ended with a polite, but firm demand, for a full explanation for and full disclosure of, the sub-probe's encrypted data files.

As the transmission was received from the spacecraft in perfect English, towards expediting a response, the sub-probe first responded with a quick transmission inquiring if it was acceptable and would not be deemed as disrespectful for it to correspond in its native language of English, which would indeed expedite its ability to respond to any of the spacecraft's inquiries. The spacecraft quickly responded by first repeating that it had assimilated all of the sub-probe's on-board data and technology with the exception of the encrypted data files and that they had full comprehension of the English language construct based upon the data files they were indeed able to access. They also acknowledged their appreciation for the sub-probe's respectful diplomatic response and confirmed that for the purpose of expediting these initial exchanges of information, utilizing the English language construct was acceptable. They then once again ended their transmission with the request for a full explanation for and full disclosure of, the sub-probe's encrypted data files, as well as for the location of its home world point of origin.

The sub-probe responded by first confirming that it was understood that it was an unmanned sub-probe and that it was released by the main exploratory probe named Evad, which is also an unmanned probe and that one of the encrypted data files contained the complete specifications for and details of, the mission of probe Evad, however, the sub-probe also provided several general stats, such as probe Evad's size, modular configuration, current speed and time conversion for when it left its home world named Earth, as well as provided general descriptive information regarding the physiology of humankind. The sub-probe then also included some general information regarding the various races that inhabit the Earth, brief descriptions of its various governing entities and the cooperative mission objectives of the Deep Space Exploratory Consortium (DSEC). It then explained that the remainder of the encrypted data files contained all available data it had on-board regarding the planet Earth and included its estimate for how far away this star cluster system was from Earth's planetary system. The sub-probe then explained that to protect its home world from a potentially hostile race it might encounter, until the intentions of any encountered intelligent life forms could be satisfactorily identified, these files would remain encrypted and advised that continued unauthorized attempts at accessing these protected files, could trigger the sub-probe's auto preservation self destruction sequence. While the sub-probe knew that the spacecraft had scanned all of its data files, it then decided to re-emphasize its mission objectives by including all of its first contact protocols and peaceful exploration directives. The sub-probe then ended this response transmission with a respectful diplomatic request for more information as to who they were, where they were from, what their intensions were and most specifically, why they had relocated the sub-probe the way they did and why they were shielding their presence, as well as the sub-probe, from the inhabitants of the fourth planet.

The spacecraft then responded thanking the sub-probe for providing more detailed information regarding its encrypted files and its precautionary protocols. After a short pause, the spacecraft shut down whichever of its systems were controlling its shielding capabilities and that were preventing the sub-probe's scanners from functioning, along with transmitting notification that they wished to observe the sub-probe's technological investigative capabilities and they were granting the sub-probe permission to scan their spacecraft and its currently available systems, however, before the sub-probe began its scans, they respectfully requested the sub-probe first review the overview report they have prepared, which they immediately began to transmit and included the following:

Their species is known throughout this star cluster and by all of the contacted races within its planetary systems, as the Purpou. The name of their home world, which is located in the planetary system closest to this system that they and the sub-probe are currently in, is Purpoun. Their species is a bi-pedal, quad-gender humanoid race, consisting of male, female and two non-gender specific genetically engineered races, one that has been specifically engineered for the purpose of labor related services and the other, for the specific purposes of the humankind equivalent of law enforcement and military personnel. While the male and female genders are surprisingly similar in appearance, size and weight as that of humankind, the genetically engineered genders are on average .61 meters taller and physically much heavier and stronger. Onboard the spacecraft is approximately 170 personnel consisting of a mixture of all four genders, with the majority of the male and female gender personnel consisting primarily of scientists. The Purpou are members of an alliance of planets that spans a multitude of planetary systems and consists of member races from one or more planets from every star system of this star cluster, except for this current system, which is the most distant system from all of the others in this star cluster and is not only the furthermost system from any of the other systems that any of the alliance races have traveled thus far, but it is also the final planetary system within the entire star cluster to be explored by the alliance. The only planet within this system currently inhabited by native intelligent life forms is the fourth planet from this system's central star. The inhabitants of this planet have named their world Blucroc. The Blucrocians are a dual-gender bi-pedal humanoid race. They are small in stature with both genders averaging .85 meters in height. The Blucrocians are an extremely intelligent, highly technologically advanced species. Their most unique physical characteristic is their one large eye, which is located in the center of the top of their head, providing them with 360° peripheral vision. The planet Blucroc rotates on its polar axis, which is nearly perpendicular to its orbital plane around this system's central star, once every sub-probe timekeeping equivalent of 43.1 hours. It is a dimly lit world due to its distance from its central star and its atmosphere, which maintains a thick cloud cover, is composed primarily of carbon dioxide and water vapor. Due to the planet's thick cloud cover there are no optical telescopes located on the surface of the planet, however, there are several small optical telescope platforms which maintain a low planetary orbit just above the planet's cloud cover and two larger, more sophisticated optical telescope platforms, which maintain geostationary orbital positions located at opposite sides of the planet at its precise equator. The Blucrocians have performed both robotic remote exploration as well as Blucrocian piloted missions to both the third planet, as well as this fifth planet, however, they currently maintain no permanent presence anywhere other than on the surface of their home world. The deep space research lab located on the planet Blucroc began final testing of the propulsion system for their new spacecraft, which will allow the Blucrocians to travel outside of their own star system. The Blucrocians are unaware of life outside of their own. The alliance of planets in their star sector have begun discussions regarding first contact. The monitoring of their progress by the alliance will continue. As the Purpou are the alliance member race whose home world is located the closest to this planetary system, they have been assigned by the alliance member races full responsibility for the monitoring of the Blucrocian's progress and for maintaining the alliance's first contact protocols. As the alliance's first contact protocols are very extensive and are deemed imperative by the alliance that they be strictly adhered to, the Purpou then respectfully requested that the sub-probe limit its scans to their spacecraft and this fifth planet and that the sub-probe also not launch any of its mini-probes until the Purpou clearly understand the sub-probe's technological investigative capabilities and have complete access to all of the sub-probe's encrypted data files, so as to be able to ensure they have a complete understanding of the sub-probe's mission objectives and exploratory intent. The Purpou ended this transmission by suggesting that the sub-probe first review the alliance's first contact protocols, as the non-detection of their spacecraft and the sub-probe by the Blucrocians is paramount until such time as that the alliance authorizes first contact. The spacecraft then immediately transmitted the alliance's first contact protocol data file to the sub-probe.

As suggested, the sub-probe first reviewed the alliance's first contact protocols and found them surprisingly similar to the first contact protocols established for probe Evad and its sub-probes by the DSEC, specifically, the directives for the non-interference in the natural development of any encountered alien life forms. Upon completing its review of their first contact protocols, the sub-probe elected to first scan the spacecraft. The sub-probe's scanners were able to scan the entire spacecraft with the exception of the central core of the craft, a section of the craft roughly 16 meters in diameter, nor were they able to penetrate a multi-faceted, pyramid-shaped dome, located at the top of the craft in line with this core, its base roughly the diameter of the core and a height of precisely twice its diameter. The spacecraft, huge in comparison to the sub-probe, has an outer surface comprised of several hundred thousand octagon-shaped tiles with a molecular composition similar to the carbon composites that were once used as a part of the heat shields of planet Earth's spacecrafts during the late 20th and early 21st centuries. The sub-probe was unable to determine the spacecraft's method of propulsion or identify its power source, nor was it able to determine how the spacecraft was generating the extremely powerful magnetic field that enveloped it, as well as the sub-probe. As the sub-probe's enhanced secondary scans were also unable to scan the central core of the spacecraft, nor identify any kind of main power source, the sub-probe could only speculate that these systems were contained within the protected core section of the craft. During the enhanced secondary scans of the spacecraft, the sub-probe's linguistic compilers completed its initial evaluation of all of the data files the spacecraft had provided access to. All indications, based upon the evaluated data files, are that the Purpou are indeed a peaceful species. Among the data files are extensive reports indicating that this fifth planet, other than remnants from multiple explorations by the Blucrocian robotic crafts, as well as obvious signs of Blucrocian physical explorations of the planet's surface, this fifth planet is a lifeless, barren world with no detectable atmosphere. As the Purpou had asked the sub-probe not to launch any mini-probes and it had completed all of its possible short-range scans and the magnetic field the spacecraft was generating, that enveloped it as well as the sub-probe, was preventing the sub-probe's long-range scans of the planet Blucroc, as well as effectively had the sub-probe captured and stranded in this current orbital location within the magnetic field, the sub-probe then concluded that it had learned everything it could under its current circumstances. None of the sub-probe's scans of the spacecraft were able to detect any obvious forms of weaponry, which left the sub-probe to speculate that either the spacecraft's weapons were being hidden within the craft's central core region, which the sub-probe was unable to scan, or, as that all other scans and data file evaluations indicate that the Purpou are a peaceful species and that this spacecraft is purely a scientific exploratory craft, it has no weapons. At that point in time, now confident it had learned everything it was going to be able to learn under all of its current circumstances, the sub-probe then ran its heavily encrypted final first contact risk assessment program. While there are many factors that are taken into consideration as a part of the final first contact assessment, as it was the sub-probe that had entered their star cluster system and all actions taken by the Purpou thus far have been deemed precautionary and peaceful, the sub-probe determined that the extraordinary potential opportunities that could be realized by establishing a peaceful cooperative relationship with the Purpou, outweighed the risks associated with allowing the Purpou full access to all of its onboard encrypted files. The sub-probe then ran its protected de-encryption program allowing complete access to all of its onboard systems and data files. When all systems confirmed access ready status and all data file encryption had been removed from the remaining protected files, the sub-probe compiled and sent a transmission to the spacecraft informing the Purpou that complete access to all of its systems and data files was now available and closed the transmission with a respectful diplomatic request for establishing an open, long-term peaceful relationship with them.

Within seconds of sending the transmission, once again, every one of the sub-probe's systems simultaneously entered the equivalent of its full diagnostic mode. As was speculated following its initial encounter with the spacecraft, that this simultaneous comprehensive system diagnostics of all of the sub-probe's systems was attributed to the spacecraft's scanning methodology, the sub-probe took no action to interfere. Moments after the diagnostics were complete, the sub-probe received its first audio transmission from the spacecraft, which, while slightly mechanical sounding, was received in perfectly enunciated English. The entire message consisted of "Please stand by... ...must reorient orbital positioning." Immediately following the transmission, in absolute silence and with no obvious engine or maneuvering thruster utilization, the spacecraft, with the sub-probe still somehow gravitationally held in position, began to orbit the planet. Upon arriving at the opposite side of the planet, with the planet now in between the planet Blucroc and the spacecraft and sub-probe, both crafts instantly came to an all-stop at this new stationary orbital position. The moment the spacecraft and the sub-probe came to an all-stop, a purple-colored ball of energy of some kind appeared in orbital alignment with the spacecraft and the sub-probe located just over 800 meters further distant from the planet. Seconds later, the ball of energy expanded spherically outwardly in a brilliant purple flash, which quickly dissipated to non-existence, then revealing another enormous spacecraft, nearly three times the overall size and mass as compared to the Purpou spacecraft. The sub-probe then detected a series of transmissions between the two spacecrafts consisting of an extraordinary volume of data. Just as the sub-probe's linguistic compilers were about to begin translating the first transmission between the two spacecrafts, the sub-probe began receiving another audio transmission from the original spacecraft.

The Purpou explained that the spacecraft that had joined them in orbit is one of their interstellar transport spacecrafts that has been sent to expedite the delivery of the replacement research and exploratory spacecraft, that has been assigned to resume their craft's mission and ultimately make first contact with the Blucrocians when agreed to by the alliance. The Purpou then explained that as their craft had made first contact with the sub-probe and their crew had extensive first hand knowledge of all of the sub-probe's systems, as well as had begun the information exchanges with the sub-probe, their mission objectives had been changed and they were now assigned the sole mission of the alliance's liaison to the sub-probe. The Purpou then stated that as it was estimated that it would be some time yet before first contact would be made with the Blucrocians and that they would be happy to share that event with the sub-probe when it takes place, they wished to extend an invitation to the sub-probe to return with them to their home world Purpoun, where a more open exchange of information would be possible, as well as where the Purpou could then also facilitate introducing the sub-probe to all of the other alliance races. The Purpou then ended this transmission by suggesting that to expedite the journey to Purpoun, the sub-probe allow them to bring it onboard their interstellar transport spacecraft and travel with them.

The sub-probe then responded by first thanking the Purpou for their invitation as this type of discovery and information exchange was indeed one of its major mission objectives. As the most critical process of probe Evad's and its released sub-probe's missions is to maintain and transmit regular report transmissions back to planet Earth via the Communication Relay Pods, the sub-probe then explained that as it did not have the onboard capability of fabricating additional Communication Relay Pods and that it had limited storage capacity, it would need to return to this system on a regular basis, or establish another means of relaying its report transmissions. The sub-probe ran multiple simulations to determine if it could utilize its various mini-probes to reroute and extend its ability to transmit, however, the distance between this planetary system and the Purpoun planetary system is simply far too vast. The sub-probe included the simulations with this transmission and ended the transmission with a respectful inquiry regarding the possibilities of regular transports of the sub-probe back to this system so it could send its report transmissions, or if the Purpou had any alternative solutions to the sub-probe's limited transmission capabilities.

Moments after sending the transmission the sub-probe received an audio transmission from the Purpou simply stating "Evaluating... ...please stand by." The sub-probe once again detected a series of transmissions between the spacecraft and their interstellar transport spacecraft and 44 minutes after receiving the stand by audio transmission, an area the size of nearly the entire bottom of the transport, glowed with the same purple-colored field as when it appeared. When the field dissipated, the same sized area of the bottom of the transport, as that of the field, was gone. A spacecraft, physically identical to the original craft that made contact with the sub-probe, exited the transport, through its now open bottom, along with an object nearly the size of the sub-probe. The exiting spacecraft maneuvered in between the transport and the sub-probe and released the object, placing it in the same orbital alignment with the original spacecraft and the sub-probe. The new spacecraft then maneuvered into an orbital position around the planet and then orbited out of view. Just as the sub-probe was about to scan the object the new spacecraft had placed in orbit, the sub-probe received another audio transmission from the original spacecraft.

The Purpou explained that the new spacecraft was the replacement research and exploratory spacecraft sent to take over their original mission. They then explained that the object that has been placed in orbit by them is a transmission relay amplifier similar to what is in common use by the alliance to maintain communication transmissions in between the various planetary systems of their star cluster system. They have programmed this one to recognize the sub-probe's data structure and would provide a second one in orbit around Purpoun when they return that will link to this one. They then stated that while they had scanned all of the sub-probe's systems and were aware of the existence and purpose of the sub-probe's Communication Relay Pod, based solely upon the sub-probe's data files and star charting methodology, they were unable to triangulate its precise location. As knowing the precise location of the Communication Relay Pod was necessary to complete the programming of their transmission relay amplifier, they provided the sub-probe with a digital audio file and asked the sub-probe to include the file as a part of a transmission to the Communication Relay Pod so that they could monitor the transmission and subsequently then be able to triangulate its precise location.

The sub-probe sent a short transmission to the spacecraft, first thanking the Purpou for their assistance with providing the access to their transmission relay amplifier and then advising that it was going to scan the device, so as that it could then include the general scan data along with the transmission as well, preparing the Communication Relay Pod for the upcoming transmission technology discrepancies that it may detect due to the utilization of the transmission relay amplifier. The sub-probe then initiated its full series of short-range technological scans of the transmission relay amplifier. The sub-probe's scans had full access to all of the transmission relay amplifier's systems and while much of its technology was beyond the sub-probe's comprehension, its transmission transponder systems were configured nearly identical to that of the Communication Relay Pod. Upon completing its scans, the sub-probe then elected to take this opportunity to also include a complete status update as a part of the transmission. When the sub-probe had completed compiling the transmission, it sent the Purpou an audio transmission advising that it was ready to transmit. The Purpou quickly responded with the one word audio response of "monitoring". The sub-probe then established its link with the Communication Relay Pod, prefacing the extensive transmission it had compiled, with a brief advisement of the underlying purpose of the transmission and the included Purpou digital audio file. Upon receiving the Communication Relay Pod's link acknowledgement and relay ready status, the sub-probe initiated the compiled transmission.

Immediately following the completion of its transmission to the Communication Relay Pod, the sub-probe received an audio transmission from the spacecraft notifying the sub-probe that as they had anticipated, by monitoring the sub-probe's transmission with their included digital audio file, they were indeed able to triangulate the precise location of the Communication Relay Pod and that it would now be possible for them to complete the configuration of their transmission relay amplifier. They then respectfully requested that the sub-probe refrain from performing any scans of any kind, nor transmit any form of communication signal of any kind, as any of which could interfere with the necessary configuration programming. They then stated that during the configuration process, it may be necessary for them to access the sub-probe's communication and transmission systems and that the sub-probe should not interpret that access as attempts on their part to communicate, making it clear, that when they complete the configuration, they would contact the sub-probe with an audio transmission clearly indicating that the process was indeed completed. They then stated that they had no way to estimate the amount of time it would take to complete the configuration of the transmission relay amplifier, but that they would give the task their highest priority towards completing the process as quickly as possible. They then ended the transmission respectfully requesting that the sub-probe shut down any unnecessary systems, so as to eliminate as much potential interference as possible and to acknowledge when it is ready for them to proceed. The sub-probe completely shut down all non essential systems and placed all secondary systems into full standby mode, leaving only its communication systems, including the linguistic compilers, the short-range and long-range scanner systems and its base power generation and distribution systems, the only systems remaining at full power. The sub-probe then sent the Purpou an audio transmission, once again thanking them for their assistance and then acknowledging that it was ready for them to proceed. The Purpou responded with the one word audio response of "initiating".

The sub-probe received the audio transmission from the Purpou acknowledging that they had completed the reprogramming and configuration of their transmission relay amplifier, which had taken 103 minutes to complete. The Purpou then stated that the sub-probe could now power up all of its systems and when ready, respectfully requested that the sub-probe send a test transmission to the Communication Relay Pod, which should now be possible by simply sending the transmission to their transmission relay amplifier. When the sub-probe completed the power up and diagnostic sequences of all of its systems that it had either shut down or placed in standby mode, rather than simply sending a generic test transmission, the sub-probe decided to take the opportunity to send a standard report transmission. When the sub-probe had completed compiling its transmission, which included the full review of the cooperative efforts undertaken with the Purpou to configure their transmission relay amplifier for the sub-probe's use, as well as included the notification that this transmission was indeed the first transmission utilizing their device, the sub-probe sent an audio transmission to the Purpou notifying them that it was ready to transmit. The Purpou responded instructing the sub-probe to align its transmission transponder directly to the coordinates of the transmission relay amplifier, as it has been programmed and configured to function identically as if it were the Communication Relay Pod and it will then, in real time, automatically transfer all transmissions directly to the sub-probe's original Communication Relay Pod.

As instructed, the sub-probe realigned its transmission transponder to the coordinates of the transmission relay amplifier and initiated the normal uplink sequence for opening communications with the Communication Relay Pod. The sequence transpired flawlessly, with the transmission relay amplifier functioning nearly transparently, causing a mere 1.43 millisecond delay communicating with the Communication Relay Pod. When the uplink had been established, the sub-probe initiated the send of the compiled report transmission. The entire transmission was sent without a single data packet error. Upon completing the transmission, the sub-probe sent an audio transmission to the spacecraft advising the Purpou of the error free process of communicating with the Communication Relay Pod and once again thanked them for providing and allowing the utilization of their transmission relay amplifier. The Purpou then responded with an audio transmission inquiring if the sub-probe was ready to accompany them back to their home world, the planet Purpoun, to which, the sub-probe responded it was and asked if it needed to take any actions to prepare for the journey. The Purpou sent the short audio response of "no... ...please stand by."

The spacecraft, with the sub-probe still held in position, then maneuvered below the interstellar transport spacecraft and slowly ascended into the enormous craft. Upon coming to an all-stop position, below the spacecraft and sub-probe appeared the brilliant purple energy field. Within seconds, the energy field dissipated and the spacecraft and the sub-probe were immersed in total darkness.

18

Frame Station

Seconds after the Purou liaison spacecraft and the sub-probe were immersed in total darkness, the brilliant purple energy field once again appeared below them. When the energy field dissipated, the bottom of the interstellar transport spacecraft was once again gone. The Purou liaison spacecraft, with the sub-probe still held in position within its magnetic field, slowly descended from within the interstellar transport spacecraft. Once they were clear of the interstellar transport spacecraft, the Purou liaison spacecraft maneuvered to a spatial positioning parallel with the interstellar transport spacecraft and precisely 43.59 meters distant from it. Upon establishing this all-stop positioning, the sub-probe then detected a rapid exchange of transmissions between the Purou liaison spacecraft and the interstellar transport spacecraft. The moment the transmissions ended, a transmission relay amplifier slowly descended from within the interstellar transport spacecraft and then maneuvered into the parallel alignment with the interstellar transport spacecraft, the Purou liaison spacecraft and the sub-probe, coming to an all-stop positioning the exact distance from the sub-probe as the sub-probe was from the Purou liaison spacecraft. The sub-probe was unable to determine if the transmission relay amplifier maneuvered into position on its own, or if it was placed into position by the interstellar transport spacecraft or the Purpou liaison spacecraft. When the transmission relay amplifier came to its all-stop positioning, the bottom of the interstellar transport spacecraft once again glowed with the purple energy field, which upon dissipating, revealed that the bottom of the craft was once again solid. Immediately following a singular short transmission exchange between the interstellar transport spacecraft and the Purpou liaison spacecraft, the interstellar transport spacecraft was enveloped in a spherical purple energy field, that rapidly shrunk in size to a brilliant ball of energy approximately one meter in diameter and with a final dissipating flash, it and subsequently the interstellar transport spacecraft, was gone. The sub-probe then received an audio transmission from the Purpou liaison spacecraft.

The Purpou notified the sub-probe that they had removed the magnetic masking field that was maintaining the sub-probe's position, as well as was masking its power signatures. They then informed the sub-probe that while the sub-probe was now free to scan and maneuver as it wished, as they had been assigned by the alliance to be their liaison to the sub-probe, their main mission was to assist the sub-probe in any manner possible and towards that end, had prepared an orientation data file for the sub-probe's review. They ended the transmission by respectfully requesting that the sub-probe confirm when it had completed its overview and initial evaluation of the orientation data file and then immediately began transmitting the file.

The orientation data file includes extensive details about the Purpou race and their revered status among all of the alliance members, as they are not only the oldest race of all of the alliance members, but they are also the most technologically advanced. The orientation data file also includes a detailed star chart map of the entire star cluster system and all of its planets. The star chart map alone is so extensive the information it contains would have taken the sub-probe years to compile. The data file also includes detailed physiological data of the Purpou race, including historical references describing their race's evolution from a dual-gender species, to their current quad-gender population and their respective societal hierarchy. Extensive data regarding their home world Purpoun is also included. The planet Purpoun is roughly 1.5 times the size of planet Earth and approximately half of its surface is a form of liquid water. Much of the land surface of the planet is composed of amethyst, which due to the light reflection of this system's star, the clouds and the atmosphere of the planet maintains a deep purple hue. There are two large Moons, which are astonishingly similar, that are gravitationally locked in precise geostationary positioning with the planet's rotation at the exact opposite sides of the planet in perfect alignment with the planet's equator. This unusual orbital relationship prevents either Moon from rotating on its own axis, resulting in the same side of both Moons constantly facing the planet. This unusual orbital relationship also makes both Moons permanent, seemingly stationary fixtures, in the skies of both sides of the planet. The Purpou have given their two Moons the names Purpougardoun and Purpougarddou. On the surface of both Moons, only on the sides of the Moons that face the planet Purpoun, are substantial populations, primarily consisting of the two non-gender specific races. While there are also male and female Purpou on the surfaces of the Moons, they are primarily scientists and research personnel. Also located on the surfaces of both Moons are large bases, equivalent to planet Earth's military installations that are responsible for protecting and maintaining the security of the planet Purpoun. In orbit around the planet Purpoun construction has reached the end of phase-one, the completion of the framework of their first space station. This circular space station, in geostationary orbit above the planet's largest landmass, will rotate on its own central axis at a rate of speed which will generate its own internal gravity equal to that of the planet. When completed, it will be the largest known artificial gravity space station ever constructed. The station is in direct alignment with the planet and the Moon Purpougardoun. The primary purpose and function of the space station will be to build and deploy the alliance's first deep space exploratory spacecrafts, which will be the beginning of the alliance's first space explorations outside of their own star cluster systems. The Purpou ended the orientation data file with the advisement that the transmission relay amplifier, that was now also in the geostationary orbital alignment of Purpoun along with the space station, had already been programmed and configured with the direct relay link to the first transmission relay amplifier that was placed in orbit around the fifth planet of the Blucrocian system and they respectfully suggested that the sub-probe send a test transmission, in order to confirm the communications link is properly synced to facilitate the sub-probe's communication transmissions to its Communication Relay Pod.

Immediately upon completing its initial scan and overview of the orientation data file, the sub-probe sent the Purpou liaison spacecraft an audio transmission first thanking them for transporting it to their home world and then for providing it with the incredibly detailed and extensive orientation data file. Once again the sub-probe determined that rather than just sending a test transmission, as the orientation data file contained such a comprehensive overview of the Purpou, their home world Purpoun and the star chart mapping of the entire star cluster systems, it would certainly be deemed by the DSEC to be a historic moment for the mission of probe Evad and its sub-probes to receive such a comprehensive report regarding confirmed extraterrestrial life. As the orientation data file was such a comprehensive overview of the Purpou, their home world and their alliance star systems and it was prepared and transmitted to the sub-probe specifically to assist with its exploration, the sub-probe determined that to ensure that there would be no misunderstanding of its intent, the sub-probe would respectfully first request permission from the Purpou to include the orientation data file as a part of its report transmission. The sub-probe then prepared the opening statement for its planned report transmission, that it would precede the orientation data file with, which included a brief overview of what the file is and the gracious manner in which it was provided to the sub-probe by the Purpou. The sub-probe then sent an audio transmission to the Purpou respectfully requesting their permission to include their orientation data file in its report transmission and included a copy of the opening statement file for their review.

The Purpou responded thanking the sub-probe for explaining its intent and gave their permission for the sub-probe to include their orientation data file in its report transmission. The sub-probe then realigned its transmission transponder to the coordinates of this second transmission relay amplifier now in orbit of Purpoun and initiated the normal uplink sequence for opening communications with the Communication Relay Pod. Just as was the case with the first transmission when utilizing the single transmission relay amplifier, which is still in orbit of the fifth planet of the Blucrocian system, this transmission sequence while utilizing the two linked transmission relay amplifiers, also transpired flawlessly and was sent without a single data packet error. Amazingly, even at this great distance from the Blucrocian system, there was still only the identical 1.43 millisecond delay communicating with the Communication Relay Pod while utilizing the two linked transmission relay amplifiers, as there was during the last transmission when only the single transmission relay amplifier was utilized. Upon completing the transmission, just as the sub-probe was about to perform a more in-depth review of the orientation data file, so as to learn more about the planet Purpoun and the Purpou race, it received an audio transmission from the Purpou.

The transmission advised the sub-probe that an envoy from every alliance member world was en route to Purpoun to personally observe and evaluate the sub-probe. There is now great excitement and anticipation amongst all of the alliance member races, as the sub-probe's visit has proved intelligent life does indeed exist outside of their own star cluster systems. Along with the envoys en route to Purpoun, every alliance member race has also begun sending additional equipment, supplies and personnel to Purpoun to assist with the next phase of construction of the space station. During this transmission from the Purpou, two spacecrafts, each nearly three times the size of the Purpou liaison spacecraft joined the sub-probe and the liaison spacecraft in orbit. The Purpou then explained that while both spacecrafts were military crafts and were heavily armored and equipped with a multitude of sophisticated weapons, one of the two spacecrafts was going to act as an alliance member conference host location for all of the incoming alliance member envoys. The mission objective of the second military spacecraft is to coordinate the orbital insertions of all of the incoming envoy spacecrafts, as well as provide overall security for the alliance member envoys as they transport from their respective spacecrafts to the Purpou conference host spacecraft. A third military spacecraft, as well as another spacecraft identical to the Purpou liaison spacecraft, then also entered orbit and positioned themselves within close proximity to the space station. The Purpou then explained that the mission objectives of these two spacecrafts are to provide security for and coordinate the second phase of construction of the space station. The Purpou then advised that they had prepared another orientation data file, which contains a brief overview of all of the alliance member races that they believe would be helpful to the sub-probe for communications purposes as the alliance member envoys arrive. They then also gave the sub-probe permission to include this data file as a part of one of its upcoming report transmissions. The Purpou ended this transmission notifying the sub-probe that in order to expedite the proper translations of all communications between it and the alliance member envoys on board the conference host spacecraft, all questions and responses should be relayed through them on board the liaison spacecraft. All alliance member races have been notified of this communication protocol and the Purpou respectfully requested that the sub-probe communicate accordingly as well.

The sub-probe sent an update transmission to the Communication Relay Pod, including the new orientation data file, thanked the Purpou for all of their assistance and advised it would review the data files while awaiting the alliance envoy arrivals.

.19
The Floating Purple-Yellow Flower Patch

Probe Evad detected a yellow dwarf star, roughly 1.7 times the size of planet Earth's sun, exhibiting clear signs of supporting a planetary system, however, due to probe Evad's distance from the system and extremely unusual gravitational distortions, the exact number of planets can not be determined. As probe Evad's long-range scans have detected faint signs of both bio-life as well as structured electromagnetic signals, a Level 3 sub-probe was fabricated and dispatched to investigate.

When the sub-probe reached full long-range scanner capable range, it activated its first contact observational protocols and engaged its propulsion system to de-accelerate to its all-stop initial observational satellite position. Upon achieving its all-stop positioning, the sub-probe initiated the start-up sequences for all of its systems that were placed in power conservation mode when the sub-probe was dispatched by probe Evad. When the sub-probe had completed all of its system diagnostics, it performed its initial series of long-range scans of the system, which yielded a great deal of information about this system, including the underlying cause of the extremely unusual gravitational distortions that were detected by probe Evad. The system consists of seven planets. Six of the planets are maintaining an elliptical orbit around the central yellow dwarf star, in nearly perfect alignment, in six unique orbital planes. The six planets are all approximately the same size, each roughly 2.86 times the size of planet Earth's Moon and their orbital planes are on average only 10,000 kilometers apart from one another. The orbital planes of the six planets are slightly arched in relation to one another due to the gravitational pull of the system's central star. The six planets and the central star are in a gravitational tug of war as the planets orbit the star, which while en route to the system made the central star appear to wobble back and forth. The average perihelion of the orbital plane of the six planets is 741 million kilometers and their average aphelion is 862 million kilometers. The seventh planet orbits more closely to the central star and also maintains an elliptical orbit. However, this planet's orbital plane is offset from the orbital planes of the other six planets by approximately 41° and its entire orbital plane also rotates around the central star due to the extremely powerful gravitational forces generated by the outer six planets. The average perihelion of the orbital plane of this single planet is 207 million kilometers and its average aphelion is 246 million kilometers. The single planet is also the largest of the seven planets and is nearly the size of planet Earth with an average circumference of 34,100 kilometers. Long-range scans detected no signs of bio-life of any kind, nor any form of technology on the surface, or in orbit of any of the six outer planets. However, long-range scans detected a wide range of bio-life on the surface of the inner seventh planet, as well as various signs of technology. No form of technology has been detected in orbit of the inner planet nor have any type of spacecrafts been detected anywhere within this system. All of the structured electromagnetic signals, as were originally detected by probe Evad, are all emanating from the inner seventh planet as well. While the electromagnetic signals have clear structure consistent with communication signals, due to distortion interference being caused by the extremely powerful and unusual gravitational forces within the system, as well as the sub-probe's current distance from the system, the sub-probe's linguistic compilers have thus far been unable to formulate a definitive language construct so as to be able to reliably translate any of the signals. Upon completing all of its long-range scans, as the sub-probe has been unable to clearly identify the bio-life on the surface of the single inner planet, nor definitively identify or translate any of the signals emanating from the planet, the sub-probe began running flight simulations towards positioning itself as far away as possible from the inner planet, yet placing it within its short-range scanner range, as well as minimizing the potential for it being detected by the bio-life on the surface of the planet speculated to be intelligent life forms.

Upon completing its evaluations of a multitude of flight simulations, the sub-probe determined that the extremely powerful gravitational forces being generated by the outer six planets would make establishing and maintaining an orbital position anywhere along the orbital plane of the six planets not only too dangerous, but due to the continual course corrections that would be required to maintain its positioning within their constantly fluctuating orbital path, the sub-probe would exhaust its fuel reserves extremely rapidly. The sub-probe then ran a series of simulations based upon approaching the inner planet from below the orbital plane of the outer six planets in a fly-by trajectory of the inner planet. These simulations indicated that this planet approach should allow the sub-probe to perform short-range scans of the inner planet towards determining the sophistication of the technology that has been detected on the planet's surface, as well as determining the level of intelligence of the detected bio-life. Should the short-range scans determine that insufficient technology exists for detecting or observing the sub-probe, the sub-probe could then initiate an orbital insertion maneuver and establish a stable orbit around the planet. If the short-range scans detect sufficient technology indicating that the potential exists for detecting or observing the sub-probe, the sub-probe would then maintain the fly-by trajectory, minimizing the possibility of it being detected and the trajectory would then allow the sub-probe to establish a long-range scanner capable range all-stop positioning located on the opposite side of the system relative to its current location. Upon completing its final trajectory calculations the sub-probe brought all of its short-range scanner systems online and while currently out of their range, the sub-probe targeted and dedicated all of the short-range scanner systems towards the inner planet. The sub-probe then targeted and dedicated all of the long-range scanner systems towards the inner planet as well and while en route, the sub-probe will focus all of its scanner and evaluative systems exclusively on the inner planet. During the fly-by trajectory the sub-probe will have an eight-day window in which it will be possible for it to alter its course towards initiating and achieving an orbital insertion of the inner planet. When all of the short-range scanner system diagnostics were complete and all navigation and flight systems had confirmed mission ready status, the sub-probe engaged its propulsion system and embarked on its fly-by trajectory of the inner planet.

At just beyond 104 million kilometers of the orbital path of the outer six planets, at which point the sub-probe was beyond the primary gravitational fields of the outer planets, both its long and short-range scanner systems began getting clear readings from the inner planet. The sub-probe focused its long-range scanners on the electromagnetic signals emanating from the surface of the inner planet, while the linguistic compilers worked on identifying and translating any potential language constructs. Simultaneously, the sub-probe focused its short-range scanners towards identifying the technology and the bio-life that has been detected on the surface of the planet. The sub-probe would have four days to scan and evaluate its findings before it reaches the point in its flight trajectory marking the beginning of its eight-day window for possible orbital insertion of the planet, of which, the third day has been identified as the optimal point of the sub-probe's flight trajectory in which to initiate and most safely accomplish the orbital insertion.

The short-range bio-life scans have identified a wide range of plant and animal bio-life on the surface of the planet, as well as in the liquid water that covers roughly half of the planet's surface. A bi-pedal humanoid species has also been detected inhabiting only two of the planets several hundred landmasses. These two landmasses are located within the general equatorial region of the planet's surface and are connected at a single point by a long artificial floating bridge roughly .8 kilometers in length. The bridge is constructed primarily from the logs and branches of the native trees. The initial round of bio-life scans has estimated that the total population of the humanoid species is approximately 300 million inhabitants. This round of bio-life scans has also determined that the inhabitants are a dual-gender species and the surface of the planet is co-inhabited by a vast array of animal life forms. The initial round of technological scans has determined that while the inhabitants are clearly an intelligent species, they appear to be technologically at a relatively primitive stage of development. Their general habitats are constructed from various combinations of the native elements, primarily the trees, soil and rock. A number of larger structures have been detected constructed primarily of block shaped rock. On both of the inhabited landmasses quarries have been detected where the rock is being excavated and the blocks are being produced. No heavy industrial equipment or facilities have been detected anywhere on the planet's surface and while the initial scans have detected clear signs of a form of electrical power, the initial scans were unable to determine how it is being generated. No form of mechanized mass transportation has been detected anywhere on the surface of the planet or in its skies.

The initial round of long-range scans of the planet have determined that the electromagnetic signals emanating from the planet are being generated by some form of communication systems being utilized by the inhabitants on the planet's surface. The communication signals are strikingly similar to the radio wave transmission signals utilized on planet Earth. The sub-probe's linguistic compilers have completed their initial evaluation and have assembled and translated this world's language constructs. The inhabitants have named their world Invishu. A series of transmissions have been detected and translated that reference a pending historic monumental journey that the inhabitants are in the final stages of preparation for. Several references indicate that a large watercraft is being constructed and the historic journey pertains to a specialized crew of inhabitants that is preparing to embark on an exploratory mission in search of additional landmasses. Based upon the volume of transmissions that have been translated thus far, the inhabitants have never traveled beyond the two currently inhabited landmasses, are unaware of the existence of any other landmasses and therefore have no understanding of how vast their world is. Additionally, the inhabitants are not aware of, nor have any comprehension of, life outside of their own world. While a number of transmissions make mention of researchers and scientists, thus far all references to their activities have been regarding various forms of surface-based technology and the preparation of the exploratory watercraft. Thus far, no references have been found regarding the stars or space in general. The only references are those speculated to be regarding this system's central star. The inhabitants use three phrases to identify either the position of the central star or the respective time of day during their daily cycle. The closest English translations of these phrases is start bright, up bright and end bright, speculated to be their way of identifying humankind's equivalent of sunrise, high noon and sunset. As the sub-probe has indeed determined that none of the detected technology is being utilized to monitor the planet's skies or the cosmos, it should be able to orbit the planet without being detected by the planet's inhabitants. As the humanoid species has only been detected inhabiting the two landmasses, the sub-probe elected to initially establish a geostationary satellite orbital positioning directly above these two inhabited landmasses. This orbital positioning will allow the sub-probe to continually monitor the activities of the inhabitants throughout the planet's entire daily rotational cycle.

When the sub-probe reached the first day of its eight-day window for initiating an orbital insertion maneuver, it ran a series of simulations towards finalizing the optimal angle for its planet approach and establishing its elected geostationary positioning. After completing its evaluations of the simulations, the sub-probe determined that the third day of this eight-day window was still the optimal timing for exiting its fly-by trajectory and altering its course towards the planet. Based upon the simulations, at precisely 3 hours and 41 minutes into the third day of the eight-day window, the sub-probe increased power to its engine in conjunction with engaging its maneuvering thrusters and altered its course to intercept the planet. Due to the sub-probe's velocity, it would be necessary for it to orbit the planet four times in order to sufficiently reduce its speed to facilitate it establishing the all-stop geostationary positioning above the two inhabited landmasses. As the sub-probe reached the planet's outer gravity well, it rotated its trajectory positioning 180° and increased its engine output to full power initiating its braking and orbital insertion maneuvers. As per the simulations it had run, with its chosen angle of planet approach, the sub-probe was easily captured by the planet's gravity well. To ensure that the inhabitants of the planet would not accidentally witness the sub-probe in the skies, it disengaged its main engine as its orbit brought it to within potential view of the inhabited portion of the planet's surface. During its fourth orbit of the planet, following its final main engine braking burn, the sub-probe's velocity had been sufficiently reduced allowing it to utilize only its maneuvering thrusters to achieve its all-stop geostationary satellite orbital positioning directly above the two inhabited landmasses. When its geostationary positioning had been stabilized, the sub-probe began its enhanced short-range scans of the planet's surface.

The initial round of enhanced short-range bio-life scans confirmed that the inhabitants are a dual-gender species and that roughly one forth of the planet's population have been identified as offspring. The inhabitants have populated the surface of the two landmasses in primarily single-family dwellings, interconnected by a series of narrow walkways and roadways constructed of soil and gravels. The majority of the single-family dwellings are constructed of the native trees, soil and rock. The enhanced short-range technological scans have determined the manner in which the inhabitants are producing their power. Built into the roofs of every dwelling on the surface of the planet are various sizes of solar panel collector and power generation units. There are no main power plants, nor are there any type of interconnected power grids. Each dwelling is self-sustaining and independently generates all of its own power needs. Located in random locations throughout the single-family dwellings there are larger habitats constructed of blocks quarried from the native rock. The larger structures vary in size from habitats supporting 10 to 20 inhabitants, to very large habitats that are capable of supporting several thousand inhabitants. Some of the largest structures have been identified as schools, manufacturing facilities, distribution centers, civic support and a multitude of commercial support habitats. Just as is the case with the single-family dwellings, all of the larger habitats are also self-sustaining and each independently generates all of its own power needs. The roofs of some of the largest habitats are nearly completely covered with solar panel collectors and their power generation units are nearly the size of one of the single-family dwellings. The combination of the solar panel collectors and their power generation units are perpetual, non-polluting sources of power. While none of the larger facilities could be classified as heavy industrial facilities in the traditional sense, several of the larger facilities produce an enormous volume of materials and goods utilized by the inhabitants including food production, clothing, building materials and small, six-wheeled solar panel powered vehicles, analogous to the small electric automobiles utilized on planet Earth. The small solar panel powered vehicles are also constructed primarily from the native trees and utilize a series of wooden dowels, wooden gears and hand woven cloth belts to propel the vehicles. The roofs of the vehicles consist of solar panel collectors just like the habitats. The power generation units mounted on the back ends of the vehicles are very similar to, albeit much smaller versions of, the power generation units utilized by the habitats, and the vehicles, just like the habitats, are self-sustaining and independently generate all of their own power needs, while generating no pollutants of any kind. The precise methodology for how the power generation units are converting the collected solar energy into the various forms of power being utilized, or how the power is being dispersed, is as of yet unknown. Until the sub-probe was able to perform its enhanced short-range scans of the surface of the planet, the combination of the non-polluting nature of the power generation and the thus far non-detection of any known form of metals being utilized by the inhabitants, led the sub-probe to speculate that the inhabitants of Invishu were in their early stages of development. The sub-probe's continuing monitoring of the Invishu communications has determined that this is not entirely the case.

While the inhabitants of the planet Invishu have only populated a small portion of their world they have developed and are indeed utilizing some extraordinary technology. The sub-probe has thus far only been able to determine that the solar panel collectors are being molded from sap collected from the native trees, however it has not been able to determine how the actual power is being generated. The enhanced technological scans have also discovered that the inhabitants are quarrying the native rock with the use of high intensity laser beam cutting tools. As is the case with their methodology for their power generation in general, the sub-probe has thus far been unable to determine how the laser beam cutting tools are being powered. A number of large rock block structures have been identified as scientific research facilities. Each facility appears to specialize in one particular area of research and the sub-probe's enhanced scans have identified the key facility responsible for the development and fabrication of the solar collectors and power generation units. The sub-probe has placed a mini-probe in geostationary orbit with it, which will be dedicated to monitoring the activities of this one facility towards learning how this technology works. Another facility has been discovered that is dedicated to the study of the native plants, trees and food production. Transmissions from this facility have also been translated which appear to be civic announcements that describe a variety of medicines developed from the native plants. A series of transmissions from this facility have also described some unusual plant life phenomenon that a team of scientists is actively researching. Amongst the vibrant green vegetation of the equatorial region of the planet Invishu patches of flowers were discovered that emanate a quiet high-pitched sound as their petals defy the planet's gravity and float within their surrounding vegetation. As there are no stems connected to, or supporting the flowers, the planet's scientists continue to study the flower patches in order to try to determine how the flowers are germinated and sustained. It is also still unknown whether it is the flowers, or the surrounding vegetation that produces the sound that these patches of flowers generate. While the surrounding vegetation of these patches of flowers is a vibrant green color, as is the majority of the vegetation of the equatorial region of the planet's surface, the vegetation that surrounds these particular patches of flowers is more the density and texture of rock, rather than that of typical vegetation. To the research scientists, while understanding how the flowers are being germinated and sustained is of key interest, it appears that the underlying mission of the research facility is to determine and find a way to artificially duplicate, the flower petal's ability to defy gravity. Another significant facility that has been detected as a result of the initial enhanced short-range scans of the planet's surface, which is also the largest facility detected thus far, has been determined to be the main communication facility for all of Invishu. This facility is also responsible for the fabrication of the communication devices utilized by the inhabitants. The devices are spherical, all roughly three meters in diameter and are composed of primarily the sap from the native trees and rock dust that is generated as a result from quarrying the rock blocks. Detected within the spheres is some form of power source, which the sub-probe speculates is responsible for the electromagnetic pulses that each are emanating. One of these spheres is attached to the top of every one of the power generation units attached to every habitant on the surface of the planet. Adjacent to this facility are a series of smaller facilities, each roughly the size of four single-family dwellings, which have been identified as data communication storage facilities, all of which, are somehow made accessible to every habitat on the surface of the planet through the electromagnetic pulses emanating from the spherical communication devices. As it has been determined that these adjacent facilities contain enormous historical archives of the Invishu research, the sub-probe has released two additional mini-probes into geostationary orbit, that will be dedicated to scanning, translating and studying the archived research towards expediting learning as much as possible, as quickly as possible, about the inhabitants of the planet Invishu.

The sub-probe's enhanced short-range scans also located the watercraft facility where the inhabitants are building the exploratory watercraft. The sub-probe released one last mini-probe into geostationary orbit with it, that will be dedicated to observing the inhabitant's progress with the watercraft's construction and its subsequent exploratory mission. The sub-probe will continue to scan the surface of the planet and monitor the interactions between the inhabitants until the mini-probe that is monitoring the watercraft facility detects the inhabitants are ready to launch the exploratory watercraft. As there have been no indications that the inhabitants of the planet Invishu have detected the sub-probe, the sub-probe will suspend any attempt at first contact until it can gain a more thorough understanding of their technology and clearer understanding of their level of intelligence and awareness as a species.

Iroti –The Quansette Nebulae

Probe Evad detected a spatial disturbance and an extraordinary volume of varied structured communication signals. Probe Evad's long-range scans also detected readings consistent with spacecraft activity within the spatial sector of the location of the disturbance. As the volume of the communication signals was so varied in constructs, probe Evad concluded the most logical explanation is that the signals are being generated by a multitude of different races. Probe Evad formulated an enhanced sub-probe tandem-array configuration utilizing five Level 3 sub-probes as it had in the past. This array however was additionally enhanced with several additional support modules. Once again, due to the complexity of and danger associated with assembling such a large array of sub-probes within its gravitational tow field, probe Evad reactivated the docked small robotic assembly unit. When the assembly unit had completed the merging of the fifth and final sub-probe into the array, probe Evad then began fabricating the additional support modules. As the support modules have no form of propulsion systems of their own, it was necessary for the small robotic assembly unit to retrieve each one from the fabrication bay as they were fabricated. As probe Evad did with the first five sub-probe tandem array, the only sub-probe that was significantly altered was the one centrally located, which rather than being equipped with its normal compliment of mini-probes, probe Evad enhanced all of its processing and control systems with additional, greater capacity sub-systems, for the coordinated control of the other four sub-probes of the array. The small robotic assembly unit attached and integrated the additional support modules to the exteriors of the four outer sub-probes of the array. A total of 16 additional support modules have been added to the array which includes; four modules to enhance the processing speed of and extend the range of the communications systems; four modules to enhance the processing speed of and significantly improve the linguistic compiler's ability to utilize each of the four compilers of the outer sub-probes in tandem, allowing the central control sub-probe to access all four of the outer sub-probe's compiler systems simultaneously, which would then allow the linguistic compiler system of the central control sub-probe, to be dedicated to data look-ups and retrievals, subsequently increasing the sub-probe's translation and communication capabilities exponentially; four modules to enhance the overall range of both the short, as well as the long-range scanner systems, which along with adding additional processing power, will cut the necessary time it will take to perform nearly all of its available types of scans approximately in half; and four modules were added to slightly extend the distance of and more than double the strength of, the sub-probe array's electrostatic force field. As enhancing each of these four key systems utilized four support modules, the small robotic assembly unit attached and integrated one each, of all four types of modules, to each of the outer four sub-probes. The support modules for the enhancement of the array's electrostatic force field, were placed on the inside sides of the four outer sub-probes facing the central control sub-probe. This positioning allowed the additional power being generated by the four support modules to be focused on strengthening the electrostatic field surrounding the central control sub-probe, providing maximum protection for the control sub-probe, should any of the outer sub-probe's sustain any type of damage. The additions of these support modules are also simultaneously slightly expanding the volume of the overall encompassing force field around the entire sub-probe array. When the small robotic assembly unit had finished its integration of the final support module, it re-docked with probe Evad and once again powered itself down into stand-by mode. Probe Evad then ran final diagnostics on all of the sub-probe array's systems and ran its final flight trajectory simulations. When complete, probe Evad uploaded its initial flight and mission directives to the central control sub-probe and began the final preparations for the sub-probe array's release. Once all of the sub-probe array's systems had confirmed they were at mission ready status, probe Evad ran its final communication tests to ensure that all five of the array's Communication Relay Pods were properly synchronized. When the final communication test was complete, due to the large mass and volume of the sub-probe array, so as to maintain the integrity of probe Evad's flight trajectory and minimize the potential for a collision with the array during its release, probe Evad began to slowly disengage the gravitational tow field initiating the sub-probe array's gradual stable fallback positioning within the tow field. When the array had reached the outer limit of probe Evad's gravitational tow range, it disengaged the tow field and the sub-probe array embarked on its mission to investigate the detected spatial disturbance.

When the sub-probe array had reached its enhanced long-range scanner capable range of the detected spatial disturbance, it initiated its braking maneuver and came to an all-stop positioning so as to perform its initial scans. The sub-probe array's initial enhanced long-range scans detected that the central region of the spatial disturbance exhibits all of the primary indications of being a black hole, however, the spatial sector of the disturbance is completely void of any stars, planetary bodies, or spatial debris of any kind. As was speculated by probe Evad, the sub-probe array's initial enhanced long-range scans have confirmed the presence of a multitude of spacecrafts within, as well as entering and exiting the spatial sector of the disturbance. Due to the extreme distance the sub-probe array was from the spatial sector at this time, while an enormous volume of apparent communication signals have been detected, it was not yet possible for the array's linguistic compiler systems to filter out, or identify within the signals, any individual structured language constructs. The enhanced long-range technological scans also detected what appears to be nearly 100 spacecrafts in stationary positions forming a large ring of crafts approximately 138 million kilometers in diameter. Due to the extraordinary volume of spacecraft activity within the spatial sector, the sub-probe array will approach this sector at half of its normal system entry velocity. The sub-probe array's linguistic compiler system has assembled a peaceful mission greeting transmission utilizing every language construct in its current linguistic database. When the sub-probe array's communication systems were fully operational, it began the looped greeting transmission, targeted all scanner systems, engaged its propulsion systems and embarked for the spatial sector at half velocity.

Just as the sub-probe array had reached normal long-range scanner capable range of the spatial sector and begun its preliminary long-range scans, 10 spacecrafts of various configurations were detected en route towards the sub-probe array. Towards attempting to be exhibiting a peaceful posture, the sub-probe array came to an all stop positioning and redirected the greeting transmissions, as well as all of its scanning systems, towards the en route spacecrafts. At their current velocity, the spacecrafts would intercept the sub-probe array in approximately 17 hours. Enhanced long-range scans of the crafts has determined that all 10 spacecrafts are unique configurations and are constructed of a wide range of materials. Based upon these unique configurations and the linguistic compilers initial evaluations of the communication transmissions, by and between the spacecrafts, the 10 spacecrafts represent 10 unique extraterrestrial races. Thus far, the intercepted transmissions have only included 10 unique language constructs; with no one language construct being utilized by all 10 spacecrafts. While there was simply insufficient time for the sub-probe array's linguistic compilers to thoroughly evaluate all 10 language constructs prior to the estimated time of arrival of the spacecrafts, the linguistic compilers were able to isolate four of them that were believed to have been sufficiently evaluated towards providing reliably accurate translations. The linguistic compilers immediately translated the sub-probe array's greeting transmission into each of the four identified language constructs and included opening diplomatic statements expressing the hope that the language was being properly translated and used. The sub-probe array then began sending the greeting transmission in only these four languages, each along with the greeting message in English, towards the attempt of identifying its own unique language construct for the spacecrafts to evaluate.

Within moments of the end of the first loop of the sub-probe array's newly translated greeting transmissions, all communications by and between the 10 spacecrafts ceased. Within a few minutes, the sub-probe array began receiving four unique response transmissions, one in each of the four newly translated language constructs. Each one of the transmissions ended with a request of the sub-probe array to respond to this message in only its own language and to send back a response transmission consisting of only an exact translation of this message, so that they could evaluate the level of the array's comprehension. Other than this request, all four of the transmissions consisted of basically the same message, "hold position until our arrival at your location". The sub-probe array's linguistic compiler translated each of the four transmissions into English, as while each message was similar in content, there were sufficient enough differences between them that the sub-probe array deemed they warranted separate unique responses. The enhanced long-range scans were also able to identify which of the 10 spacecrafts sent the four unique transmissions, as well as which spacecrafts each of the four transmissions originated from. When the linguistic compiler had completed translating all four messages, the sub-probe array's communication systems targeted the four identified spacecrafts and sent each one their respective response transmission. Within minutes of completing the transmission, the sub-probe array received a transmission from each of the four spacecrafts, all of which sent in English and this time, all were precisely identical in content, which was the following; "please state mission objective and intent regarding your approach of galactic node". As thus far the sub-probe array's linguistic compiler has found no other references to a galactic node, it responded by transmitting its standard first contact detailed mission briefing, in both data, as well as audio formats and ended the transmission by inquiring if the spatial disturbance, which the sub-probe array now speculated to be some type of exhausted or dormant black hole, was what they were referencing as a galactic node. Within minutes, once again the sub-probe array received a short transmission, this time consisting of audio only, in English, which simply stated, "evaluating... ...hold position until our arrival your location". The sub-probe array responded with a short audio "standing by" message. Just as the array had completed this confirmation transmission, the 10 spacecrafts had traveled within the array's short-range scanner range. The sub-probe array immediately began its initial round of enhanced short-range scans of the 10 spacecrafts.

One of the spacecrafts is approximately three times larger than the other nine crafts and all nine of the spacecrafts are considerably larger than the sub-probe array. As originally detected by the long-range scans, all 10 spacecrafts are constructed of a wide range of materials and while each is emitting its own unique propulsion and power signature, an unusual overall power signature has been detected encapsulating all 10 spacecrafts and all 10 crafts are traveling at precisely the exact same velocity. Now that the spacecrafts have traveled within short-range scanner range, the linguistic compilers have now been able to distinctly identify the 10 individual language constructs, expediting the translation of the transmissions. Each of the nine spacecrafts is processing and utilizing, on average, only two to three of the 10 total language constructs that have been detected, only the single largest spacecraft is processing and utilizing all 10. The spacecrafts are en route to the sub-probe array traveling in a formation with the large spacecraft in the center, with the nine smaller crafts encircling it; all positioned precisely 91.44 meters away from the central large craft. As the spacecrafts would arrive at the location of the sub-probe array in just under six hours, the sub-probe array continued to translate and evaluate as many of the 10 language constructs as possible within the available timeframe. As a precaution, prior to the arrival of the 10 spacecrafts, the sub-probe array compiled a complete update report transmission of all that it had learned thus far and transmitted it to its Communication Relay Pods. While en route to investigate the spatial disturbance, other than its main Communication Relay Pod, which was placed within the flight trajectory of probe Evad when the array was dispatched, the sub-probe array has thus far released only one other of its four remaining Communication Relay Pods. Based upon the signal strength of this most recent report transmission and the sub-probe array's calculations of the distance the spatial disturbance is from the array's current location, to maintain the signal strength and the integrity of its report transmissions to the main Communication Relay Pod, the sub-probe array will need to release one more of the remaining three Communication Relay Pods while en route to the spatial sector of the detected disturbance.

The 10 spacecrafts arrived and came to an all-stop positioning precisely 914.4 meters away from the sub-probe array. The moment they achieved their all-stop positioning, the sub-probe array began receiving an audio transmission, in perfect English, from the large central spacecraft. The inhabitants of the central craft introduced themselves as the Quansette. They stated that based upon the comparisons of all of the recorded histories of all of the known life forms that have thus far been encountered; their species is the oldest known race. As their level of technology also far surpasses that of any of the known races, the Quansette have taken on the role, which has the closest English translation of, protector. The Quansette then stated that the closest English translation of the name that has been given to the association of all of the races that are present and participating in the explorations utilizing the galactic node would be, companions. The Quansette acknowledged that they had processed the information that the sub-probe array included in the mission briefing it had provided and appreciated the general information, but they now required full disclosure of its systems capabilities, complete mission directives and all available data regarding the physiology of its occupants and species. Before the sub-probe array even had the chance to respond, an extremely intense beam of light emanating from the Quansette spacecraft enveloped the sub-probe array. The beam of light repeatedly vacillated through the colors of the spectrum and during the entire time the sub-probe array was enveloped by the light, every one of its systems was in a state of total suspension. When the Quansette disengaged the light beam, the sub-probe array received a communications ping from the Communication Relay Pods seeking to re-establish their communication link with the sub-probe array. Upon re-establishing its communication link with the Communication Relay Pods, the sub-probe array ran a communication synchronization diagnostic and discovered that there was precisely a 10 hour difference in time coding between the array and the Communication Relay Pods, indicating that the sub-probe array had been incapacitated for 10 hours.

Just as the sub-probe array began to compose a transmission to ask the Quansette what had transpired, the array began receiving another audio transmission from them. The Quansette began this transmission by declaring that they had scanned and evaluated all of the sub-probe array's systems and data files and have determined that its mission objectives and intent is indeed of a peaceful exploratory nature. They then stated that they were intrigued to learn that the array was an uninhabited spacecraft and that it and probe Evad had traveled so far from their home world Earth in the manner in which they have. The Quansette then stated that after completing their entire system scan and evaluation of the sub-probe array's systems and data files, they now had a thorough understanding of humankind's language constructs and level of technological achievement and would from this point forward, communicate with the sub-probe array entirely in English, translating all names and references to humankind's closest equivalent. While they were a little concerned regarding what was learned about humankind's violent past, based upon the sub probe array's historical data files, they were going to give humankind the benefit of the doubt. The Quansette then requested, that as onboard their spacecraft was a representative of every companion race that is collaborating on the research and utilization of this spatial sector's galactic node, that the sub-probe array should communicate any inquiries it might have, only to this spacecraft, until the sub-probe array's language and data system constructs have been evaluated and translated by all of the companions onboard this craft. Due to the magnitude of the gravitational fields of this galactic node, the Quansette then instructed the sub-probe array to notify their craft before the launch of any of its onboard mini-probes so as that they could first review its mission objective and then monitor its progress. A number of forms of experiments around and within the galactic node are strictly prohibited and the onboard companion counsel will transmit the full list of what those are, as soon as the translation to English has been completed. The Quansette then informed the sub-probe array, that as the volume of data available regarding the galactic node far surpassed the storage capacity of the sub-probe array's data file storage systems, immediately following this transmission, they will transmit a data file they have assembled and translated, providing the sub-probe array with an overview of what is known about the galactic nodes and how the companions are utilizing them. The Quansette then stated that they would escort the sub-probe array to the galactic node, provided flight trajectory and velocity parameters they wished the sub-probe array to maintain while en route and instructed the array to engage its engines when ready. The Quansette spacecraft then immediately began to transmit the overview data file to the sub-probe array. While the transmission was being received, the sub-probe array's navigational systems prepared the necessary programming for the requested flight trajectory and velocity, refocused all of its long-range scans on the spatial disturbance and when all systems diagnostics confirmed mission ready, the sub-probe array engaged its engines and embarked along the Quansette's provided course.

The overview data file that the Quansette has provided the sub-probe array with, is an enormous wealth of information, not only regarding the spatial disturbance, but contains extensive reference segments pertaining to all of the companion races as well, including basic language translation guides for all of their main communication languages. The sub-probe array, confident that the DSEC would deem the overview data file to be of extraordinary value, it began to prepare the extensive data file for transmission to the Communication Relay Pods. As the sub-probe array was preparing the transmission, it tested the signal strength between it and its two currently deployed Communication Relay Pods and determined that to ensure the integrity of this, as well as future transmissions, it was time to deploy another of its three remaining Communication Relay Pods. The sub-probe array then sent a transmission to the Quansette spacecraft advising it of its plan to deploy the Communication Relay Pod and requesting confirmation that it was safe to do so, as well as wanted to confirm it was acceptable to the Quansette and companion races, that it forward a copy of the overview data file back to Earth. The Quansette immediately responded advising the sub-probe array that it was indeed safe for it to deploy the Communication Relay Pod and that it was acceptable to all of the companions for the array to forward a copy of the overview data file to its home world. When the sub-probe array confirmed that the communication relay processors had been properly reconfigured, now incorporating this third Communication Relay Pod to be deployed by the array, it released the Communication Relay Pod deploying it without incident. As soon as the newly deployed Communication Relay

Pod had achieved a stable all-stop positioning, the sub-probe array began transmitting the overview data file. When the transmission data stream had reached its maximum relay speed, the sub-probe array began further evaluation of the overview data file, specifically focusing its research on all data segments that reference a galactic node.

The provided data segments that reference the galactic node have confirmed that the spatial disturbance is indeed a variant of an exhausted black hole that has collapsed in on itself and due to the extraordinary magnitude of energy that was expelled at the moment of its collapse, an oscillating gravitational well was created that alternately merges with a series of other similarly collapsed black holes located within a multitude of nearby galaxies. These recurring intergalactic mergings are enormous gravitational tunnel formations, which exert such massive gravitational forces upon one another during their merged cycle that they cause the rotational spin direction of their event horizons to constantly alternate in direction. Once merged, the opposing spin directions of the two merged collapsed black holes causes the gravitational tunnel formation between them to twist and distort itself to the point of snapping apart at its precise center. Once separated, the two gravitational tunnels collapse back to their respective black holes, at which point they are immediately gravitationally jettisoned back out until they merge with the next gravitational tunnel in their respective sequence of partnered black holes. It has been determined from the ongoing study and utilization of the black hole in this spatial sector by the companion races, that this black hole has exactly 1,000 partner black holes in its recurring merging sequence. Due to the extreme vastness of the Universe and incalculable number of galaxies, it is unknown at this time if every black hole of this type has the same quantity of partner black holes, however, every galaxy that has been explored by the companion races thus far, has at least one of this type of collapsed black holes and as many as 10 have been discovered in a number of the larger galaxies. It is also still unknown how or why this black hole maintains the identically recurring merging order with its 1,000 partner black holes. The ongoing research being performed by the companion races has however confirmed that the merging cycle of all of the partner black holes is precisely equivalent to 10 Earth hours. It was nearly 100,000 Earth years ago that the Quansette first discovered and began its research of these intergalactic phenomena and took them thousands of years of research experiments to discover and confirm the recurring cycle they maintain. Shortly after the Quansette discovered the recurring cycle, they began experimenting with attempting to send probes through the gravitational intergalactic tunnels that are being created. These experiments eventually led to the now commonplace traversing of these intergalactic tunnels with inhabited spacecrafts. Countless lives from all of the companion races have been lost during the ongoing pursuit to traverse these gravitational intergalactic tunnels. While there are references to hundreds of races that have visited, examined and participated in missions to traverse these intergalactic tunnels, thus far, only the 10 races that are currently escorting the sub-probe array have developed spacecrafts that have successfully traversed one or more of the intergalactic tunnels and returned safely. The spacecrafts that the sub-probe array's enhanced long-range technological scans initially detected, which form the large ring of crafts encircling the black hole, have now been identified as all being Quansette spacecrafts. The initial scans, due to the gravitational distortions being generated by the black hole and the ring of spacecrafts, also caused an incorrect approximation of the diameter of the ring that the crafts form. Instead of the 138 million kilometers as initially approximated, the ring of Quansette spacecrafts has been confirmed to be precisely 100 million kilometers in diameter and consists of exactly 100 Quansette spacecrafts. The precise positioning and purpose of the ring of spacecrafts has also now been confirmed. The 100 Quansette spacecrafts that make up the ring are each generating extremely powerful electromagnetic gravitational fields, allowing each spacecraft to gravitationally link to its neighboring spacecrafts, forming the stationary gravitational ring, with each spacecraft located a mere 1,000 kilometers from the black hole's event horizon. The positioning of this stationary gravitational ring of spacecrafts allows the Quansette and guest companions onboard, to continue their ongoing research of the partnered black holes, which the companions refer to as galactic nodes, as well as gives them the ability to continuously monitor their recurring merging cycles. Their positioning also allows them to monitor all communications with the probes and spacecrafts currently located in the partnered galactic node galaxies. Due to the precise 10-hour merged cycles of the 1,000-partnered galactic nodes, the available 10-hour communications windows between the ring of Quansette spacecrafts and the probes and spacecrafts currently located in the partnered galactic node galaxies, each cycles every 416.6 Earth days. The ring of spacecrafts also provides gravitational and navigational assistance to any probe or spacecraft wishing to traverse any of the intergalactic gravitational tunnels the merged partnered galactic nodes creates, by providing all necessary data as to which pair of galactic nodes in its cycle are actively merged and all critical timing references as to when the various gravitational tunnels are considered stable and safe to traverse. Just as the sub-probe array was about to review a data segment containing a listing of all of the probes and spacecrafts currently stationed in partnered galactic node galaxies, it began receiving a transmission from the Quansette spacecraft.

The Quansette informed the sub-probe array that they were approaching the critical approach maneuver distance from the galactic node and requested that the array come to an all-stop positioning. When the sub-probe array and the 10 companion escort spacecrafts came to an all-stop positioning, the Quansette then explained that due to the varying and extremely powerful gravitational forces being generated by the galactic node, it was necessary to approach the node utilizing a very specific flight trajectory and coordinating the approach with the ring of Quansette spacecrafts, so as to safely achieve a stable parked positioning close enough to the galactic node's event horizon for mission staging and not be accidentally and inescapably drawn into it. The nine companion spacecrafts encircling the Quansette spacecraft all engaged their engines and embarked for the galactic node. The Quansette spacecraft then informed the sub-probe array that to assist and ensure that the array would safely achieve a stable parked positioning within the galactic node's mission staging range, they were going to gravitationally link with it and escort it to a proper staged positioning. The Quansette spacecraft then slowly maneuvered to within 100 meters of the sub-probe array, at which point an intense beam of light emanating from the bottom of the Quansette spacecraft, similar to the initial scanner beam that was used, enveloped the sub-probe array. However, this beam of light remained a consistent translucent red color, as opposed to vacillating through the colors of the spectrum as did their scanner beam and while the sub-probe array was completely enveloped in the light, all of its systems and scanners also remained online and fully functional, unlike when the Quansette spacecraft initially scanned the array. The Quansette then confirmed that a gravitational link had been established with it and then told the array not to engage any of its propulsion systems unless specifically instructed to do so by them, as that now that their spacecraft and the array were gravitationally linked, doing so could cause their two crafts to potentially catastrophically veer off course. The Quansette spacecraft then engaged their propulsion systems and they, with the sub-probe array in gravitational tow, embarked for the galactic node mission staging perimeter zone.

The Quansette spacecraft followed a flight trajectory that at precisely 1,000,000 kilometers from the event horizon of the galactic node, the flight trajectory was then perfectly parallel to and in perfect plane alignment with the galactic node's event horizon, at which instant, the Quansette spacecraft disengaged its propulsion systems. With the Quansette spacecraft and the sub-probe array still in gravitational tow, then in a momentum glide path towards the ring of Quansette spacecrafts, an extraordinary volume of ultra high speed data communications were detected between the escort Quansette spacecraft and the ring of Quansette spacecrafts encircling the galactic node. Without any propulsion activity by the escort Quansette spacecraft, its velocity began to rapidly decrease until it and the sub-probe array came to an all-stop positioning precisely 100,000 kilometers from the galactic node's event horizon. The moment the all-stop positioning was achieved, the sub-probe array began receiving an audio transmission from the Quansette escort spacecraft while both its short and long-range scanner systems began receiving a flurry of scan result notifications. The Quansette informed the sub-probe array that it was no longer gravitationally linked to their spacecraft and that its current positioning was now being monitored and maintained by their research scientists and their galactic node mission coordinators aboard the Quansette spacecrafts encircling the galactic node. They then advised the array that they would follow this transmission with a data file containing all of the critical flight trajectory parameters for entering and exiting this galactic node mission staging perimeter zone and that to ensure the array's safety, as well as the safety of all of the other spacecrafts within the staging perimeter zone, it was imperative that the sub-probe array precisely follow these flight trajectory parameters and only exit and enter the zone after first establishing final timing and positional coordinates with the galactic node mission coordinators. The Quansette escort spacecraft then informed the sub-probe array that they had uploaded their entire scan and interaction data archives that they have compiled thus far regarding the array to their research and mission coordination data processing network. They then advised that as they were scheduled to replace one of their research spacecrafts currently located in a partnered galactic node galaxy, they would remain in their current location and would be available to assist the sub-probe array until their two target galactic nodes have stably merged. The sub-probe array then began receiving the data file containing the flight trajectory parameters from the Quansette escort spacecraft.

While the sub-probe array's communications and linguistic compiler systems processed the Quansette's data file transmission, the array began its review and evaluation of the short and long-range scan result notifications that were activated when this current all-stop positioning was first established. Due to the volume of scan result notifications that were received when this current all-stop positioning was established, while the sub-probe array was receiving some short and long-range scan result notifications while it was encapsulated within the Quansette escort spacecraft's gravitational tow beam during their flight escort to this galactic node mission staging perimeter zone, it is apparent that the field that was created by their tow beam had still significantly interfered with and delayed the processing of the scans the sub-probe array had initiated while en route. Due to the sub-probe array's current position, parallel with the galactic node's event horizon and the plane of the encircling Quansette spacecrafts, the array's scan view field is limited to approximately half of the ring of spacecrafts and the mission staging perimeter zone, beyond which, the gravitational distortions being generated by the ring of spacecrafts, as well as those emanating from the galactic node, are interfering with the array's ability to scan any further. The array's long-range scans were now able to determine that the Quansette spacecrafts that encircle the galactic node that are within its scanner capable range, are identical to one another and are roughly four times the size of the escort spacecraft. While the gravitational linking fields being generated by each of these spacecrafts are similar in appearance to the tow beam that was generated by the Quansette escort spacecraft, the gravitational forces they are generating are exponentially more powerful. The gravitational fields they are producing are not only maintaining their stationary positioning around the galactic node, but they also extend outwardly from the ring of spacecrafts creating and maintaining the mission staging perimeter zone, all of which, has the same translucent red color as did the Quansette escort spacecraft's tow beam. The sub-probe array's short-range scans have detected hundreds of varying configurations of spacecrafts within the mission staging perimeter zone ranging from stationary research crafts, to staged spacecrafts awaiting their clearance and assistance from the galactic node mission coordinators to enter the galactic node. The sub-probe array then sent a transmission to the Quansette escort spacecraft inquiring as to what the proper procedure and protocol is for launching a probe into the galactic node, as it would like to dispatch one of its mini-probes so as to gather some first-hand data of one of the gravitational tunnel formations that are formed when two partnered galactic nodes merge.

Rather than receiving a response from the Quansette escort spacecraft, the sub-probe array began receiving an audio transmission, in perfect English, from the ring of Quansette spacecrafts encircling the galactic node. Neither the sub-probe array's short, or long-range scans, could determine which of the Quansette spacecrafts was sending the transmission, seemingly, the transmission was being sent by all of the spacecrafts simultaneously. The transmission began with the notification that they had reviewed and evaluated all of the data that their research vehicle, which had escorted the sub-probe array to this galactic node, had collected and uploaded to their research and mission coordination data processing network and wished to welcome the array and humankind. They then stated that based upon the data files contained within the sub-probe array's linguistic compiler's database, they would do their best to translate all communications and data files into humankind's English language and mathematical constructs. The closest English translation as to who they are is the companion cooperative. Their purpose is to protect and monitor the galactic node and to the best of their ability, ensure the safety of all of the companion races utilizing it. The companion cooperative then notified the sub-probe array that immediately following this audio transmission, they would send a data file containing all of the protocols for utilizing the galactic node, including all flight trajectory data for mission staging and galactic node traversal initiation. They ended their initial audio transmission by providing the sub-probe array with the required coordinates that it should target its main communications transponder to for all future transmissions, whether directed at them, or any companion race spacecraft located within the mission staging perimeter zone. The sub-probe array then immediately began receiving the galactic node protocol data file transmission.

Along with providing all of the required trajectory data for mission staging and galactic node traversal initiation, the protocol data file also included explanations and directives regarding the required communications procedures for sending all audio and data file transmissions. As the primary directive of the companion cooperative is to ensure the safety of the galactic node and all of the companion spacecrafts utilizing it, due to the extraordinary volume of the ongoing communication transmissions taking place and the paramount importance of the precise timing for all galactic node traversal initiations, the utilization of the single transmission conduit ensures the most efficient processing of this extraordinary volume of transmissions and minimizes the potential for interference and traversal initiation delays as much as possible. One of the most critical mandates included in the protocol data file dictates that all companion races that are scheduled to traverse any of the galactic tunnels, must engage their various systems as required so as to engage the directed galactic node initiation maneuver they are assigned and to do so precisely on time. If for any reason, a precise initiation maneuver cannot be facilitated, the scheduled spacecraft must immediately abort its scheduled galactic node traversal and return to its last assigned location within the mission staging perimeter zone. If the scheduled spacecraft is incapacitated and unable to maneuver for any reason, it must immediately broadcast a stage one emergency transmission. No companion spacecraft is to attempt to render any type of assistance to any incapacitated spacecraft unless specifically directed to do so by the companion cooperative. Quansette emergency spacecraft are on permanent alert and will coordinate any required assistance for any incapacitated spacecraft if needed. The protocol data file also includes the required flight trajectory that all companion spacecrafts must utilize to maneuver from their holding position within the mission staging perimeter zone to the traversal entry staging position, located at the precise center above the galactic node and precisely 100,000 kilometers from the galactic node's event horizon plane. This arched flight trajectory requires that all spacecrafts remain at the precise distance of 100,000 kilometers from the galactic node's event horizon at all times, except for when initiating the final segment of their actual galactic node entry maneuver. Upon completing its review of the protocol data file, the sub-probe array prepared one of its general purpose exploratory mini-probe's and when the mini-probe was confirmed mission ready, the array sent a request transmission to the companion cooperative requesting to be scheduled for an exploratory traversal mission by its currently prepared mini-probe. The sub-probe array also included as a part of its request transmission, all of the flight trajectory and velocity data it had programmed the mini-probe with.

The companion cooperative responded to the sub-probe array's request informing it that as only one companion spacecraft was currently scheduled to traverse the next galactic node merging, they have scheduled the array's mini-probe to be the second entry mission during the next merging cycle, which would begin in 4.31 Earth hours. The companion cooperative then advised that they would follow this transmission with a mission flight plan data file and that the sub-probe array should program all of the mini-probe's navigational systems as per the flight plan data file's specifications and be prepared to instantly initiate the entry maneuver when the array receives the mission initiation clearance confirmation transmission from them. The sub-probe array then received the flight plan data file. The array updated the mini-probe's navigational system's programming as per the specs provided and reviewed the included procedural lists of what actions the companion cooperative and the ring of Quansette spacecrafts were going to take to assist with the mini-probe's entry into the galactic node. At precisely the 10 minute mark prior to the scheduled mission initiation, the sub-probe array received an audio transmission from the companion cooperative advising that the first mission companion spacecraft had successfully entered the galactic node and that the array should now be in final stand-by mode awaiting their mission initiation clearance confirmation transmission. They then requested that the sub-probe array confirm that all of its systems were ready and that the mini-probe was indeed at mission ready status, to which, the array responded that all systems were ready and standing by for their mission initiation transmission. At precisely the scheduled time, the sub-probe array received the mission initiation transmission from the companion cooperative and immediately engaged the mini-probe's propulsion system. As programmed, the mini-probe followed the arched flight path maintaining its consistent distance of 100,000 kilometers from the galactic node's event horizon plane until it arrived at the traversal entry staging location, at which point it disengaged its main propulsion system and came to its all-stop positioning upon orienting itself facing the galactic node. When its all-stop positioning was stabilized, as per the flight plan data file's specifications, the mini-probe sent the companion cooperative a transmission advising them that it was in position and ready to proceed. The companion cooperative immediately responded instructing the mini-probe to engage its propulsion system and to accelerate to one tenth of its maximum velocity. When the mini-probe achieved the designated velocity, as per its programmed mission directives; it began transmitting its telemetry data targeted to the companion cooperative's communications conduit, which was instantaneously relayed to the sub-probe array. When the mini-probe was precisely 10,000 kilometers from the galactic node's event horizon plane, the translucent red glow of the gravitational ring being sustained by the Quansette spacecrafts that encircle the galactic node, pulsed in color density a single time and the mini-probe instantly accelerated through the galactic node's event horizon plane and was gone. Other than the telemetry data confirming the mini-probe's crossing of the galactic node's event horizon plane, no other data was received from the mini-probe. Immediately following a communications locator ping transmission by the sub-probe array the array received an audio transmission from the companion cooperative.

The transmission explained that moments after the mini-probe entered the galactic tunnel, it was crushed and vaporized upon veering into the tunnel wall. The companion cooperative then advised that as no other traversal mission had as of yet been scheduled for this current galactic merging, if the sub-probe array wished to attempt a second traversal with a differently configured mini-probe, they were standing by for its request. The sub-probe array then configured one of its mini-probes that was designed and fabricated specifically for exploring gravitationally turbulent conditions and when the mini-probe confirmed it was at mission ready status, the array sent the companion cooperative a transmission advising them that it was ready and included the full configuration specifications of the prepared mini-probe. The companion cooperative responded with the single word audio transmission of: "evaluating". After a brief pause, the companion cooperative advised that they had processed multiple simulations based upon the specifications provided for the prepared mini-probe and every simulation they processed resulted in the destruction of the mini-probe. Immediately following the companion cooperative's transmission, the sub-probe array began receiving an audio transmission from the Quansette escort spacecraft, via the galactic node communications conduit, that as they were scheduled to traverse the next galactic node merging, they would be willing to gravitationally protect and tow the sub-probe array's mini-probe through the next galactic node merging. The sub-probe array then determined that as the mini-probe was going to be protected by the Quansette spacecraft's gravitational tow beam, rather than sending the currently configured mini-probe, which was chosen and configured more due to its durability than its functionality, it would instead, configure one of its most sophisticated mini-probe's for the traversal mission, which has the most varied scanner systems configuration, as well as the most powerful communications system of all of the mini-probes onboard the array. When the replacement mini-probe confirmed it was at mission ready status, the array sent the companion cooperative a transmission once again advising them that it was ready and included the full configuration specifications of the replacement mini-probe that had been prepared. The companion cooperative advised the sub-probe array to stand by for a flight plan specification data file transmission. Following a number of high-speed data communications between the companion cooperative and the Quansette escort spacecraft, the sub-probe array received an audio transmission from the companion cooperative. They advised that the next galactic node merging would take place in just over three Earth hours and that the Quansette escort spacecraft was the first scheduled traversal mission and was making its final preparations. The sub-probe array then immediately began receiving the new flight plan specification data file.

Identically to the sub-probe array's first traversal mission attempt, at precisely the 10 minute mark prior to the scheduled mission initiation, the array received an audio transmission from the companion cooperative requesting that the array confirm that its mini-probe's navigational systems had been programmed as per the newly transmitted flight plan specification data file and that it and the array were mission ready, to which, the array responded that all systems were indeed ready and standing by for their mission initiation transmission. Once again, at precisely the scheduled time, the sub-probe array received the mission initiation transmission from the companion cooperative and immediately engaged the mini-probe's propulsion system. As programmed, the mini-probe came to an all-stop positioning when it reached its designated rendezvous coordinates located one kilometer from the sub-probe array. Moments later, the Quansette escort spacecraft rendezvoused with the mini-probe, came to an all-stop positioning just long enough to capture the mini-probe with its gravitational tow beam and then proceeded along the arched trajectory towards the traversal entry staging location. Upon its arrival at the traversal entry staging location, the Quansette escort spacecraft came to an all stop positioning after orienting itself facing the galactic node. Following a single brief communication exchange between the companion cooperative and the Quansette escort spacecraft, the spacecraft, with the mini-probe encapsulated within its gravitational tow beam, began to accelerate towards the galactic node. Simultaneously, the mini-probe began transmitting its telemetry data, targeted to the companion cooperative's communications conduit, which was instantaneously relayed to the sub-probe array. As was the case with the sub-probe array's first mini-probe traversal attempt, when the Quansette escort spacecraft was precisely 10,000 kilometers from the galactic node's event horizon plane, the translucent red glow of the gravitational ring being sustained by the Quansette spacecrafts that encircle the galactic node, pulsed in color density a single time and the Quansette escort spacecraft, with the mini-probe in tow, instantly accelerated through the galactic node's event horizon plane and were gone. The sub-probe array then began to receive a steady stream of scan result notifications from the mini-probe, which were being relayed to the array by the companion cooperative communications conduit, however, all standard communications with the mini-probe had stopped functioning. Just as the array began to process the scan result notifications, it received an audio transmission from the companion cooperative advising that thus far the traversal mission was proceeding as scheduled and without incident. The companion cooperative also informed the sub-probe array that it requires precisely 10 Earth minutes to traverse every gravitational tunnel created by the merging of every pair of partnered galactic nodes and complete communications with the mini-probe should be re-established once the Quansette research spacecraft, that is escorting the mini-probe, exits the partnered galactic node. The companion cooperative then ended this audio transmission by advising the sub-probe array that they would immediately follow this transmission with a mission data file consisting of overview information regarding the galactic location of this partnered galactic node, as well as the Quansette's general research mission objectives. The array then immediately began receiving the mission data file transmission.

The mission data file indicates that the primary objective of the Quansette research spacecraft is to continue the ongoing research of the Quansette Nebulae, so named nearly 20,000 Earth years ago, when it was originally discovered by a Quansette traversal mission. The Quansette Nebulae is located in the Trieotsette Galaxy. It is the most violent and subsequently the most colorful Nebulae ever discovered by the known life forms of the Universe. It is so expansive and unnavigable, that its actual size is unknown. No probe that has ever been sent to explore or map it has ever returned. The furthermost penetration by deep space scans is 11.6839 light years, at which point the turbulence and radiation becomes too extreme. It is believed by some that it is one of the barriers of an edge of the Universe. It is said, Iroti, the headless guardian of The Road Of Stars, points the way to the Nebulae's center. Iroti, named after the lead astronomical researcher that was onboard the Quansette's spacecraft that first discovered and observed the Nebulae, is an enormous stellar nursery located approximately three light years from the Trieotsette Galaxy. Approximately four light years further distant, is a counter-clockwise rotating stellar debris field with a bright white central core of stars. As stars are released by the stellar nursery Iroti, those stars that are not drawn into this rotating stellar debris field are following a course, creating a trail of stars, referred to by the Quansette as The Road Of Stars, which leads to an incalculably sized, clockwise rotating circular cluster of stars, speculated to be the center of the Nebulae. Due to the immensity of the Nebulae, the actual distance to this speculated Nebulae's center, is as of yet unknown. Moments after the sub-probe array completed its review of the Quansette's mission data file, it began receiving communication transmissions from both the Quansette escort spacecraft, as well as the mini-probe, being relayed by the companion cooperative's communications conduit.

The Quansette escort spacecraft advised that it had arrived in the Trieotsette Galaxy and had rendezvoused with the research spacecraft they are there to replace, at which point they released the mini-probe from its gravitational tow beam. The mini-probe acknowledged that all of its systems were fully operational and it began to stream its short and long-range scans to the sub-probe array, which continued to be relayed to the array by the companion cooperative communications conduit. Moments later, the Quansette research spacecraft, which had been replaced by the spacecraft that escorted the mini-probe to the Trieotsette Galaxy, came through the galactic node at an astonishing velocity, instantly arriving at and coming to an all-stop positioning at, the traversal entry staging location, oriented facing away from the galactic node. Following a series of data file exchanges between the Quansette research spacecraft and the companion cooperative, the research spacecraft, still utilizing the companion cooperative's communications conduit, advised that it was embarking for the Quansette home world and then rapidly accelerated out of this spatial sector.

While the current communications link was established with the mini-probe, the sub-probe array gathered as much real-time data from the mini-probe as it could prior to the end of the current merged cycle between this galactic node and its partnered galactic node located in the Trieotsette

Galaxy. As the sub-probe array had been advised, precisely 10 Earth hours after these two galactic nodes had merged, all communications with the mini-probe were lost. The sub-probe array immediately received an audio transmission from the companion cooperative advising that the galactic merge cycle with the Trieotsette Galaxy had come to an end, providing the array with its countdown start mark for the next merging cycle, which would begin in precisely 416.6 Earth days. As at that point the sub-probe array had collected an extraordinary volume of data, it compiled a complete report transmission and when prepared, the array sent the report transmission to its Communication Relay Pods.

As the sub-probe array's current position allows it to monitor the activities of this galactic node through the utilization of the companion cooperative's communications conduit, the array will remain in its current location and learn as much as possible about the partnered galaxies until the next merging cycle with the Trieotsette Galaxy. The discovery of this galactic node is one of the most extraordinary discoveries thus far by probe Evad or any of probe Evad's sub-probes, as it exponentially expands humankind's space exploration capabilities by providing the ability to extend the exploratory missions beyond humankind's Milky Way Galaxy.

End Of Transmission: 06.21.07.01.20

When the "End Of Transmission" time stamp appeared on all of the main communication display screens located in all of the respective DSEC Master Control Rooms, indicating the end of the first report transmission data stream from the Mainframe Communication Relay Pod, as when the transmission began, the thunderous uproar and applause in each of the DSEC Master Control Rooms, was close to deafening. The exploratory mission of probe Evad has far out surpassed its original mission objectives, as well as, has now definitively proven that humankind is indeed not alone in the Universe. The probe Evad mission was immediately deemed by the DSEC to be the single greatest scientific accomplishment in humankind's history. News of and replays of the transmission from the Mainframe Communication Relay Pod spread around the planet Earth and the settlements on the Moon and the planet Mars, in a matter of hours. The probe Evad mission brought humankind together as a species in a manner crossing all racial barriers, with humankind's realization that they truly are a single species, inhabitants from the planet they call Earth. Following several hours of independent staff meetings and conferences, the DSEC made the announcement that a mission review conference would be held on Level 8 (L 8), Main Operational Control, of the Control and Earth Relay Complex (CERC), located on the Moon, in 32 days, providing all of the nations of the Earth with sufficient time to coordinate the transport of their desired representatives to the Moon.

During the entire 32 days, as representatives and additional support personnel arrived from Earth and preparations were being made to broadcast a live feed of the mission review conference from the CERC's Main Operational Control to every nation of the Earth, as well as the settlements on the Moon and the planet Mars, there was an around-the-clock bustling of activity throughout the entire CERC. The majority of the representatives that traveled from Earth to take part in the mission review conference, coordinated their journey to the Moon and all traveled together onboard a single DSEC cargo transportation spacecraft, that was equipped with additional landing craft spacecrafts to expedite the transfer of all of the conference participants from the DSEC cargo transportation spacecraft, to the CERC on the surface of the Moon. While a number of leading scientists and the DSEC engineering team that have been installing the artificial gravity systems in the International Research Facility on the surface of the planet Mars were en route to the Moon, their transport spacecraft would not arrive at the Moon in time for this first DSEC mission review conference, however, an enhanced two-way uplink video communications feed was established between the Mars transport and the CERC's Main Operational Control, which would allow the scientists and the DSEC engineering team onboard the transport to participate in the conference in near real-time. When the DSEC cargo transportation spacecraft arrived from Earth and established its Lunar orbit, Moon Traffic Control was given full authority and control of the coordination of all of the landing craft spacecraft flights, during the transfer of all of the participants from the DSEC cargo transportation spacecraft to the CERC's main landing zone, while final preparations were still under way in Main Operational Control. While extra security personnel were placed on active duty, with the overwhelming cooperative spirit that has been inspired by the discoveries of the probe Evad mission, the majority of the security personnel acted in the capacity of personnel escorts and CERC diplomatic liaisons, assisting the participating world representatives as they arrived and reported in. The normal compliment of security personnel maintained their regular posts, ensuring the security of the CERC's critical systems and monitoring those areas of the CERC that are restricted to only properly authorized personnel. All of the landing craft spacecraft flights that took place in between the DSEC cargo transportation spacecraft and the CERC main landing zone, as well as all of the independent landing craft spacecraft flights that took place in between their respective transport spacecrafts and their related Moon settlement landing zones, all took place without incident and all conference participants arrived safely as scheduled.

For efficiency purposes, as well as for additional security and safety purposes, on the first day of the mission review conference, due to the CERC then being at its maximum personnel capacity and with the accommodations that had been made in Main Operational Control, to seat as many personnel as possible for the conference, CERC Security Operations, which is also located in Main Operational Control, had put together a schedule and coordinated the movement of all of the participating personnel from their assigned personnel quarters, to their assigned seating in Main Operational Control. As the participating personnel were reporting in to Main Operational Control, Mission Control Operations performed final communications and up-link transmission tests in preparation for the live-feed broadcast of the mission review conference. Following several hours of all of the participating personnel reporting to Main Operational Control, as instructed to do so by CERC Security Operations, all of the scheduled participants had been assembled and with all of the communications systems preparations complete, the mission review conference was ready to begin. The Director of the DSEC sat down at the CERC video communications console located in Mission Control Operations. As Mission Control Operations is located at the center of Main Operational Control and with the open, tiered-level design of Main Operational Control, everyone present could see the Director. When the Director was ready, the video feed was engaged and the Director appeared on every monitor connected to the CERC's live-feed broadcast of the mission review conference, the largest broadcast audience in humankind's history. Also connected to the CERC's broadcast feed are all of the video feeds from all of the non-secure areas of the CERC and TAC, including the exterior video feeds from the numerous permanent observational cameras on the surface of the Moon. When the Director appeared on the video monitors, all of the participants present in Main Operational Control quickly grew quiet. The Director began by saying: "Welcome all, to this historic first probe Evad mission review conference.", to which, every participant in Main Operational Control rose to their feet with cheers and applause. Following several minutes of this opening celebration and congratulatory exchanges, the Director asked everyone to take their seats and come to order. The Director began the conference with a brief historical overview of the probe Evad mission and then gave tribute to the hundreds of scientists, researchers, engineers, mission specialists and administrative personnel, that have died since the probe Evad mission and all of its support projects were begun. The Director then gave tribute to and acknowledged the remaining 143 personnel, all of whom were present in Main Operational Control for the conference, that have been a part of the probe Evad mission project since the original world meetings that led to the formation of the DSEC. Once again, all of the personnel present rose to their feet with cheers and applause. For the live-feed broadcast, video footage from the various cameras located in Main Operational Control was transmitted, as the cameras scanned the personnel during the congratulatory exchanges with the DSEC founding members. The Director then once again asked everyone to return to his or her seats and come to order. When everyone had returned to their assigned locations, the Director began a brief review of the first transmission from probe Evad's Mainframe Communication Relay Pod and outlined the agendas and research team assignments, to those personnel, now responsible for the in-depth research of the 20 individual segments of the transmission. The Director then announced, that the DSEC Project Planning Council had convened to review the receipt of the first transmission from probe Evad's Mainframe Communication Relay Pod and due to the extraordinary discoveries of the galactic node, the Quansette and the companion cooperative races, as per the 20th segment of the transmission, the Council had come to a unanimous agreement that the most logical choice for the first follow-up mission, should be a manned spaceflight mission to the galactic node. This was an announcement that would change the way in which all of the nations of the world would come together and cooperatively work together, forever. The Director ended his opening comments advising all of the conference participants of the schedule for the remaining 14 days of this first probe Evad mission review conference and then stated that the remainder of the first day would be an open forum. The celebratory reaction to the Director's opening comments, by not only the participants present in Main Operational Control, but by all of humankind, was unprecedented. The remainder of the first day of the conference was a humankind interpersonal event like no other in its history. While hundreds of independent review meetings and discussions were held, the DSEC Project Planning Council re-convened in the CERC's Level 5 Research Lab to review their initial proposed manned mission to the galactic node, which the Director was to announce during his opening comments of day two of the conference. Media coverage of the conference, was being broadcast worldwide and to all of the settlements on the surfaces of the Moon and the planet Mars, non-stop.

Due to the thorough planning and scheduling that was done by CERC Security Operations, the assembly of all of the personnel to Main Operational Control for day two of the conference, took place quickly and efficiently. When it was confirmed that all of the conference participants were present in Main Operational Control, the Director of the DSEC sat down at the CERC video communications console and welcomed everyone to the second day of the conference. The Director began with a quick review of the probe Evad mission database access that had been set up to consolidate and centralize all of the transmissions, research data files and follow-up reports, providing everyone with the complete history, as well as all of the up-to-the-minute reports for this on-going mission, located in one master database. The Director then announced that the DSEC Project Planning Council had prepared an overview briefing regarding their initial proposed parameters for the manned follow-up mission to the galactic node discovered by probe Evad. The DSEC Project Planning Council has identified this follow-up mission, as the Galactic Node Expedition (GNE). The Council has uploaded the full details of their initial proposed mission parameters to the DSEC's Research Computer Mainframe and has assigned full open database access to all of the participants. While the parameters of the follow-up mission are only in their initial developmental stages, the Director stated that the Project Planning Council wished to provide a brief overview of the proposed GNE mission and that the Planning Council welcomes any comments, or project assistance, from any of the conference participants, or world nations, that wish to take part in this historic first manned deep space mission. The Director then presented the following GNE mission overview briefing:

"The Project Planning Council has determined, based upon the flight trajectory data received from the sub-probe array that is currently stationed at the galactic node, that by utilizing the DSEC's newest, most advanced propulsion systems, it will take 28.6 Earth years for the proposed manned spacecraft to travel to the galactic node. The proposed GNE spacecraft would be developed by first assembling a tandem array of three of the DSEC cargo transportation spacecrafts and then supplementing the array with the additional support modules that will be required to transport and indefinitely support the number of personnel being proposed for its crew. For this first manned deep space mission, due to the lengthy period of time it will take to travel to the galactic node, the Project Planning Council is recommending that the crew be comprised of 100 complete families consisting of no more than four children each, this being another first for humankind's space exploration, in that it will be the first mission to consist of complete families and to include the training and active participation of children in the mission. The proposed configuration of the tandem array, would entail joining the three enormous spacecrafts together in a stacked, tiered formation, with two of them in a lower orientation, spaced apart from one another so as that the top upper decks of the two spacecrafts that face the upper spacecraft, would be connected to the lower decks of the third upper spacecraft that face each of the two lower crafts. Along with the multitude of hatches that will be installed along these main connections between the three spacecrafts, four personnel transportation conduits, large enough to support two traffic lanes for the small, six-person personnel vehicles, as well as a designated personnel walkway, would then also connect the two lower spacecrafts. Elevator shafts, centrally located in each of the four connecting personnel conduits, would then connect the conduits to the bottom of the upper spacecraft. These connecting conduits and their elevator shafts will not only provide for greater personnel movement capacity between the three spacecrafts, but they will also function as additional support trusses, providing connection stability to these three enormous spacecrafts. The two lower spacecrafts will be reconfigured identically to one another, each designed to support 50 family personnel quarters. Two of their landing craft bays will be replaced with high-efficiency hydroponics bays for natural food production and two of their landing craft bays will be converted into water recycling and water production facilities. The hydroponics bays and the water production bays on either spacecraft will have sufficient capacity to support the entire array, should any type of emergency, or maintenance situation arise with the other. The upper spacecraft of the array will be reconfigured to include all of the main command and operational control facilities, with the exception of the lower forward section of the spacecraft, which will be reconfigured into personal quarters for the GNE Mission Commander and the senior mission supervisory personnel. Two of the upper craft's bays will be converted into the array's Mission Research and Main Computer Centers, one bay will be converted into its Medical Center and one bay will be converted into the array's Main Personnel Support Services facilities including; conference rooms, private offices, supply dispensaries and all mission supervisory offices. The top two decks of the forward section of the spacecraft will be converted into the array's Main Operational Control. The rear sections of the upper spacecraft will be converted into the array's Main Engineering and Main Propulsion Coordination Operations. The exteriors of all three spacecrafts will also undergo a number of reconfigurations and enhancements. Emergency escape modules will be added to strategic external locations of all three of the spacecrafts and will be of a sufficient number to support nearly three times the number of initial personnel, to provide for personnel growth, as well as to provide for rapid access should an emergency situation arise that would require their use. All of the spacecraft's standard external communication transponder dishes will be replaced with larger and more powerful units. Similar to those used by probe Evad, the array will also be equipped with a

Mainframe Communication Relay Pod and a series of standard Communication Relay Pod's for sending all of its report and personnel transmissions back to the TAC throughout its ongoing mission. Due to the advancements in technology that have been made since the launch of probe Evad, it has not been determined as of yet how many Communication Relay Pod's will be required to support this array's mission to the galactic node. While there are thousands of such logistical details that still need to be worked out in order to construct this proposed array, by combining and reconfiguring three of the existing DSEC cargo transportation spacecrafts, the Project Planning Council has determined that this approach will save countless years towards developing and constructing a spacecraft to undertake this historic mission."

The Director then ended this briefing, given to open the second day of the conference, by recommending that everyone review the full details of the Project Planning Council's initial proposed mission parameters that have been uploaded to the DSEC's Research Computer Mainframe and then advised, that like day one, this second day of the conference would also be an open format and that the formal, structured participant discussions, would begin the following day, day three of the conference. As the Director stood up to walk away from the CERC video communications console, once again, everyone present in Main Operational Control that was not already standing, rose to their feet in thunderous exuberant cheers and applause. After several minutes of celebration and congratulatory exchanges, most of the participants, primarily within departmental groups, began their review of the Project Planning Council's initial proposed mission parameters data file, while the Director and the Council members mingled throughout all of the departments in Main Operational Control answering questions and logging participant inquiries and mission comments. The remainder of the second day of the conference was spent primarily focused on the Project Planning Council's proposed manned mission to the galactic node

Over the next 12 days of the conference, the 20 committees that had been assigned to fully review and evaluate the 20 individual transmission segments received during probe Evad's Mainframe Communication Relay Pod's first transmission, began their research while the probe Evad mission control supervisory committee continued to review and evaluate all of probe Evad's telemetry data and system diagnostics reports that were included as a part of the transmission. The Project Planning Council spent the majority of their time meeting with the various committees and the council representatives of the world's nations. They also had a number of meetings with representatives from the world's major media networks. The press and news coverage of the conference was non-stop and was continually being broadcasted around the world. During the course of the conference, the representatives from the world's major media networks repeatedly petitioned the Project Planning Council towards adding a fourth DSEC cargo transportation spacecraft to the proposed array, to be modified to support an additional 50 family personnel quarters, as well as to support the ongoing media coverage of the mission. On the 14th day of the conference, all of the representatives from the world's major media networks convened in the CERC's Level 5 Research Lab with the entire Project Planning Council, including the Director of the DSEC, to review the media network's complete proposal for adding the fourth DSEC cargo transportation spacecraft to the proposed array and to include members of the media and their families as a part of this historic crew. All of the probe Evad mission committees spent this day finalizing their reports regarding their findings and evaluations and updating all of their departmental database records in the DSEC's Research Computer Mainframe, while all of the department supervisors prepared their mission status reports for the final day of the conference. When the Project Planning Council and the Director completed their meetings with the world's major media networks, they reconvened in the Project Planning Council's main private conference room located adjacent to the Research Lab and spent the remainder of the day reviewing all of the ongoing departmental database updates and voting on the next mission directives, while the Director also prepared his presentation for opening the final day of the conference.

The 15th and final day of this DSEC mission review conference began with great expectations and excitement amongst all of the conference participants. When it had been confirmed that all of the conference participants were present, the Director once again sat down at the CERC video communications console to deliver his opening presentation. The Director began by welcoming everyone to this final day of this historic mission review conference and thanked everyone for their hard work, long hours and valued input. He then delivered the following presentation:

"Following many hours of deliberations, along with the overwhelming support from all of the world nations, the Project Planning Council has unanimously agreed, that while continuing to monitor the transmissions from probe Evad and its sub-probes, along with the continued enhancements that have been planned for the DSEC's Spaceport, as well as the continued support for the ongoing development of the facilities on the surface of the Moon and the planet Mars, the next major DSEC undertaking would indeed be the proposed manned deep space mission to the galactic node discovered by probe Evad." Main Operational Control erupted into the most exuberant round of thunderous cheers and applause of the conference thus far. Following several minutes of celebratory exchanges and non-stop applause, the Director requested that all come to order. When all of the participants had returned to their assigned locations, the applause subsided and Main Operational Control once again grew quiet, at which point, the Director then continued his presentation: "While as of today, there are countless details to be worked out regarding the implementation of a manned mission of this proposed magnitude, I wanted to begin this final day of this mission review conference, with a few updates regarding the mission that have developed during the conference. Following a series of proposal meetings with the world's media representatives, the Project Planning Council and I unanimously agreed that a fourth DSEC cargo transportation spacecraft will be added to the GNE array. In general overview, as was originally proposed for the two lower spacecrafts, this fourth spacecraft will be reconfigured with 50 family personnel quarters, with two of its landing craft bays replaced with high-efficiency hydroponics bays for natural food production and two of its landing craft bays converted into water recycling and water production facilities. The two upper decks at the front of this spacecraft will be converted into the array's main media and press support operations. Two of its bays will be converted into centralized educational facilities and two of its bays will be converted into personnel entertainment facilities. This fourth spacecraft will be added to the array by connecting the outsides of its top deck to the inside lower decks of the two main personnel support spacecrafts. The elevator shafts, centrally located in each of the four connecting personnel conduits, will be extended to connect the conduits to the top of this fourth spacecraft, which will now be the lowermost spacecraft of the array. Due to the enormous size that this finished GNE array configuration will be, it has been deemed impractical to generate artificial gravity onboard the array through any standard rotational means. This being the case, the GNE array will be the first spacecraft in humankind's history to employ the artificial gravity generation as is utilized here on the Moon and the settlements on the surface of the planet Mars. The DSEC's leading artificial gravity engineers en route to the Moon from Mars, have already begun formulating an approach for how to integrate the newest artificial gravity technologies, like those being employed in the International Research Facility on the surface of the planet Mars, into the proposed GNE array. Their greatest challenge will be the perpetual generation of the adequate power levels that will be required to generate and maintain the gravitational fields on a structure as large as the proposed GNE array. It has not yet been determined whether each of the four DSEC cargo transportation spacecrafts that will make up the array should generate and maintain their own individual gravitational support systems, or whether a singular gravitational support system should be developed to support the entire array as a whole. Similar to the other three spacecrafts, the exterior of this additional fourth spacecraft will be reconfigured to include additional emergency escape modules and will be enhanced with a series of large transponder dishes that will replace its standard communications transponder dishes. Due to the positioning of this fourth spacecraft within the GNE array configuration, the communications transponder dishes currently located on the top of this spacecraft will be removed and the series of larger enhanced transponder dishes will be mounted to the bottom of the spacecraft. As all four of the DSEC cargo transportation spacecrafts that will become part of the GNE array will undergo major reconfigurations, which will include the complete replacement of their propulsion systems, the Project Planning Council has agreed that the four oldest crafts of the current fleet of six will be utilized for the GNE array. Additionally, the first of the DSEC cargo transportation spacecrafts that was constructed, currently in Lunar orbit, will be the first to be reconfigured and will become the uppermost main operational control section of the GNE array. Its final voyage and mission as a DSEC cargo transportation spacecraft will be its return trip to Earth orbit, transporting those of you returning to the DSEC Spaceport and shuttling those of you returning to Earth. Once all of the passengers and non-essential crewmembers have disembarked from the DSEC cargo transportation spacecraft, the spacecraft will be powered down into full space-docked mode. When all pertinent systems have been powered down, the final shut down sequence will involve taking its propulsion systems off-line. Once off-line, the DSEC cargo transportation spacecraft will then officially take on its new designation as the GNE Array. The GNE Array will remain docked with the DSEC Spaceport until all of its major internal reconfigurations are complete, at which point the GNE Array will disengage from the DSEC Spaceport and then establish its own geostationary orbit parallel to the Spaceport. The GNE Array will establish its geostationary orbit far enough away from the DSEC Spaceport to safely facilitate the docking and addition of the remaining three DSEC cargo transportation spacecrafts; yet will orbit close enough to the Spaceport so as to adequately support the ongoing construction of the GNE Array. The DSEC cargo transportation spacecraft in Lunar orbit is scheduled to depart in 14 days and the shuttling of personnel from the Lunar surface to it will begin in three days. Moon Traffic Control will be issuing landing craft departure schedules and will have the schedules uploaded to the CERC's Computer Mainframe for everyone to review before the close of the conference today. The first GNE Array construction conference will take place onboard the docked GNE Array in approximately three months, following the return of the DSEC engineering team currently en route from the planet Mars, due to arrive at the Moon in 68 days. The exact date of this first construction conference will be announced once the DSEC engineering team completes their Mars mission debriefing here in the CERC's Main Operation Control and has had the opportunity to return to Earth for some much deserved personal time with family and friends, as most of them have been stationed on Mars for several years. The Project Planning Council and I will continue to keep everyone informed regarding the GNE Array's construction and its historic mission through our ongoing updates, which we will regularly upload to the DSEC's Research Computer Mainframe. While the 20 committees, that have been assigned the detailed review and evaluation of the 20 transmission segments that were a part of probe Evad's Mainframe Communication Relay Pod's first transmission, have been performing their research and uploading their findings to the DSEC's Research Computer Mainframe, the probe Evad mission control supervisory committee, while reviewing and evaluating all of probe Evad's telemetry data and system diagnostics reports that were included as a part of the transmission, have determined that the power savings that probe Evad's Mainframe Communication Relay Pod would realize by buffering the report transmissions from the released sub-probes, is not as significant as was originally anticipated. Subsequently, the probe Evad mission control supervisory committee has had multiple meetings with the probe Evad mission communications computer systems programmers and believe it would be possible to transmit a reprogramming sequence to probe Evad's Mainframe Communication Relay Pod, that will alter its transmission directives which will facilitate the instantaneous relay of the sub-probe report transmissions to the TAC here on the Moon, rather than waiting until its transmission buffer is full. Thus far, all of their calculations indicate that the power requirements for instantaneously relaying the sub-probe transmissions as they are received, may even consume less of the Mainframe Communication Relay Pod's power reserves than buffering the sub-probe report transmissions and batch transmitting them back to the TAC. The probe Evad mission communications computer systems programmers also believe that they can transmit and upload the reprogramming sequence to the Mainframe Communication Relay Pod's main communications control systems, without replacing, or interfering, with its current buffering and multi-transmission programming. This approach will ensure that if for any reason the upload of this new programming should fail, or the new instantaneous transmission release sequence not properly initiate the relay of a received sub-probe transmission, the Mainframe Communication Relay Pod's currently programmed transmission sequence will continue to initiate the sub-probe report transmissions as soon as its transmission buffers are full. By utilizing the DSEC's newest ultra high speed communication transmission protocols, the probe Evad mission communications computer systems programmers have estimated that it will take approximately three months for the reprogramming sequence to reach probe Evad's Mainframe Communication Relay Pod once transmitted from the TAC. During the most recent meeting between the DSEC Project Planning Council and the probe Evad mission control supervisory committee, it was unanimously agreed that the exact duplicate of probe Evad's Mainframe Communication Relay Pod, which has been in storage here on the surface of the Moon, that has been used for testing and evaluation in the past while awaiting the first transmission from the live Mainframe Communication Relay Pod deployed by probe Evad, will once again be placed into Lunar orbit, so that the transmission and upload of the reprogramming sequence can be thoroughly tested. The duplicate Mainframe Communication Relay Pod has already been relocated from its long-term storage location to Facility Maintenance located on Lower Level 2 (LL 2) here in the CERC. As a team of engineers have just begun the physical clean up and general systems diagnostics of the duplicate Mainframe Communication Relay Pod, it is not yet possible to estimate when it will be ready for its Lunar orbit insertion.

The engineering team assigned to prepare the duplicate Mainframe Communication Relay Pod for its insertion into Lunar orbit, will upload their progress reports to the DSEC's Research Computer Mainframe, and the DSEC Project Planning Council will announce the scheduled Lunar orbit insertion date and time as soon as it has been established. While the duplicate Mainframe Communication Relay Pod is being prepared, the probe Evad mission communications computer systems programmers will continue to review and refine the reprogramming sequence, while the probe Evad mission control supervisory committee coordinates the preparation of the DSEC's Lunar landing craft that will be used to transport the duplicate Mainframe Communication Relay Pod into Lunar orbit. This same landing craft will be configured and programmed to send mock sub-probe report transmissions to the duplicate Mainframe Communication Relay Pod, once the reprogramming sequence has been transmitted to it from the TAC and the upload of this new sequence to its main communications control systems has been acknowledged as completed. When all of the transmission tests have been completed, the DSEC's Lunar landing craft will recapture the duplicate Mainframe Communication Relay Pod and return it to the Lunar surface. Once on the surface, it will be returned back to Facility Maintenance located on Lower Level 2 (LL 2) here in the CERC for a complete systems diagnostic. If this final systems diagnostic does indeed confirm that the reprogramming sequence has been properly and permanently integrated into the duplicate Mainframe Communication Relay Pod's main communications control systems, the transmission of the reprogramming sequence from the TAC to probe Evad's live Mainframe Communication Relay Pod will then be scheduled. The DSEC Project Planning Council and I met yesterday with the DSEC Director of Personnel, who by now you all know is not only responsible for coordinating all general ongoing personnel support, but is also responsible for the final selection and subsequent training coordination of all DSEC mission personnel. As the GNE Array mission is humankind's first manned deep space mission and due to its lengthy one way travel time of 28.6 Earth years, today is deemed to be a mission of no return, it was clear that an updated series of testing and evaluation protocols needs to be developed for the selection of the mission personnel, which would now also entail for the first time in humankind's space exploration history, the inclusion of children as active members of the crew. Subsequently, in yesterday's meeting, the DSEC Project Planning Council and I requested that the DSEC Director of Personnel and his supervisory team have their initial protocol recommendations ready for our review during the upcoming first GNE Array construction conference, as mentioned previously, which will be scheduled to take place in approximately three months onboard the GNE Array. Even with the inherent danger associated with space travel and the likelihood, due to the travel time of this particular mission that the crewmembers will never again return to Earth, the DSEC has already received more than 100,000 requests from around the world from people wishing to be considered for this historic mission's crew. As it is the DSEC's desire that the crew of the GNE Array be as ethnically diverse as possible, while the DSEC Director of Personnel and his supervisory team work on the development of the updated series of testing and evaluation protocols for crewmember selection, the DSEC Project Planning Council and I will be meeting with representatives of the world governments towards facilitating the establishment of DSEC recruitment communication centers around the world, so as to make submitting a request to participate in this historic mission accessible to as much of humankind as possible. In closing, I would once again like to thank everyone for your participation in this first probe Evad mission review conference. Thanks to everyone's dedication and extraordinary efforts, not only has the probe Evad mission proven to be a resounding success, but the unanimous agreement to undertake the GNE Array mission, I believe, is the beginning of what will prove to be the most significant era in all of humankind's history. The agenda for today, the final day of this first probe Evad mission review conference, is for all departments to finalize and upload your conference directive reports to the DSEC's Research Computer Mainframe and to submit your formal recommendations for the ongoing probe Evad mission, as well as any agenda issues you would like to submit for consideration for the upcoming first GNE Array construction conference. The DSEC Project Planning Council and I will remain available throughout the day so as to address any specific questions any of you may have. Once again, thank you all for your outstanding work and dedicated participation."

As the Director stood up from the CERC video communications console, Main Operational Control again erupted with celebratory cheers and applause. For nearly an hour, everyone present mingled throughout Main Operational Control exchanging congratulatory embraces and acknowledgements. Gradually all DSEC personnel made their way back to their respective departments and resumed their summary discussions and reporting activities, while the remaining guest participants continued to mingle throughout Main Operational Control, as many responded to interview inquires from the various world media representatives that were present to cover and report on the ongoing conference activities. Throughout the remainder of this final day of the probe Evad mission review conference, all of the DSEC Project Planning Council members, as well as the Director, also mingled throughout all of the departments of Main Operational Control praising each of their individual departmental accomplishments and contributions, answering questions and documenting when all departments confirmed that their final departmental conference report uploads had been completed.

Over the next two days, while all DSEC personnel that were actively stationed at the CERC returned to their normal duty schedules, the remaining visiting DSEC personnel, the visiting world nation representatives and the participating world media representatives, all attended a number of social events held in the CERC's Food Services on Level 7 (L 7) and Entertainment Services on Level 6 (L 6), while the Lunar Landing Crafts were prepared for shuttling all of the conference participants from the surface of the Moon to the DSEC cargo transportation spacecraft in Lunar orbit. On the third day following the end of the conference, the first participants scheduled to leave the CERC reported to In/Out Processing and were then prepared and assisted with their spacesuits in Facility Entry & Exit Processing, all located in the CERC's Lower Level 2 (LL 2) and the shuttling of all of the departing personnel from the CERC to the DSEC cargo transportation spacecraft began. The first personnel to depart the CERC were the DSEC support personnel that had been assigned liaison duties to assist the visiting conference participants during the conference, as well as while onboard the DSEC cargo transportation spacecraft. During the first day of personnel departures, eight of the participating world media representatives, after each of them had gained additional pledged support for the DSEC from their respective world nations, petitioned the Director of the DSEC and the DSEC Project Planning Council for permission for four of them to remain at the CERC and four of them to remain onboard the DSEC cargo transportation spacecraft destined to be re-commissioned as the main operational control section of the GNE Array, as permanently stationed personnel so as to provide ongoing media coverage of the probe Evad mission, the construction of the GNE Array and its developing mission, as well as all of the ongoing and future support activities undertaken by the DSEC. Following a brief meeting between the Director of the DSEC and the DSEC Project Planning Council, upon their unanimous agreement, the Director instructed the DSEC Director of Personnel to issue the eight world media representatives their applicable permanent personnel quarters and to immediately schedule their DSEC operational and security protocol orientations. Over the next 10 days, the remaining visiting conference participants were safely shuttled from the CERC to the DSEC cargo transportation spacecraft without incident. The 14th day following the conference, began with a flurry of activity in the CERC's Main Operational Control as all final pre-flight system diagnostics were performed on the DSEC cargo transportation spacecraft in preparation for its departure and return flight back to Earth orbit. Onboard the DSEC cargo transportation spacecraft, as the flight crew made all final preparations for departure, a ship-wide broadcast was made instructing all non-crew member personnel to report to the main forward cargo bay to prepare for departure. The main forward cargo bay is specially configured with adequate seating and flight support equipment so as to accommodate the DSEC liaison personnel and all of the conference participants that accepted the DSEC's invitation to travel to and from the Moon via the DSEC cargo transportation spacecraft.

As all personnel reported to the main forward cargo bay, the DSEC liaison personnel once again assisted all of the conference participants with their flight spacesuits, strapping them into their assigned seats and connecting their flight life support systems. Once all of the conference participants had been prepared, the DSEC liaison personnel assisted each other with their flight spacesuits, as the liaison supervisor strapped each of them into their assigned seat, as they were ready. When all DSEC liaison personnel were ready for departure, a team of DSEC cargo transportation spacecraft flight specialists arrived to assist the liaison supervisor. Once they had strapped the liaison supervisor into his assigned seat and connected his flight support system, they then performed final inspections of all personnel and flight support systems in the main forward cargo bay ensuring all systems confirmed flight ready. When complete, they notified flight command that all systems were go for flight in the main forward cargo bay, secured all of the cargo bay hatchways as they exited and then reported to their designated flight stations. The flight commander of the DSEC cargo transportation spacecraft then notified CERC Main Operational Control that all systems and personnel have been confirmed flight ready and that they were ready and standing by for clearance for Lunar orbit departure.

The Director of the DSEC took his seat at his flight operations control console in CERC Main Operational Control and made the announcement for all personnel to prepare for final confirmations for the DSEC cargo transportation spacecraft's Lunar orbit departure. The CERC Main Operational Control quickly grew quiet as all personnel took their seats at their flight control stations. The Director then began calling out each flight control operation requesting their go, or no go, for the DSEC cargo transportation spacecraft's Lunar orbit departure. When all operations had confirmed that all systems were indeed go for departure, the Director notified the flight commander of the DSEC cargo transportation spacecraft that they were cleared for departure and wished them a safe journey back to Earth. The flight commander acknowledged and gave the order to engage all departure engines. As the enormous DSEC cargo transportation spacecraft's engines ignited and gradually powered up to full thrust, the spacecraft rapidly accelerated from its minimal orbital velocity to its required orbital escape velocity and as it broke the second horizon of the backside of the Moon, it left Lunar orbit and embarked on a perfect trajectory towards Earth. The Director of the DSEC moved from his seat at his flight operations control console to the CERC video communications console and made the following announcement:

"I just wanted to take this opportunity to congratulate everyone within the DSEC, as well as extend our enormous gratitude to all of those who have assisted the DSEC to date, as together, we have thus far achieved some truly remarkable accomplishments. While the successful departure of the DSEC cargo transportation spacecraft marks the end of this first probe Evad mission review conference, the extraordinary success of and the wealth of knowledge obtained due to the probe Evad mission thus far, along with the plans and actions agreed upon during this historic conference, particularly the agreement to undertake the GNE Array mission, truly marks just the beginning, of humankind's collective journey throughout the vastness of space..."

To follow the ongoing adventures of the

intergalactic exploratory probe Evad,

its sub-probes, the ongoing missions of

the DSEC and humankind's explorations

throughout the vastness of space...

...please visit:

www.TheWorldsOfEvad.com